EMERALD

KAREN WALLACE

EMERALD

SIMON AND SCHUSTER

First published in Great Britain in 2011 by Simon and Schuster UK Ltd,
a CBS company.

Simon & Schuster UK Ltd
1st Floor, 222 Gray's Inn Road, London WC1X 8HB

A CIP catalogue record for this book is available from the British Library.

978-1-41691-716-8

1 3 5 7 9 10 8 6 4 2

Printed and bound in Great Britain by Cox & Wyman, Reading RG1 8EX.

www.simonandschuster.co.uk

To the new Mistress of Camphire

Part One

HAWKSTONE HALL

Chapter One

"I'd rather marry a hog than Lord Suckley," I shouted at Arabella. "You told me he was a lecher and that his breath stank like a midden."

"Grow up," sneered Arabella. "That was before I knew you were to be betrothed to him."

She plucked at the brown wool of my dress. "At least he's rich – so you won't have to wear these rags any more."

"This is your mother's kirtle," I snapped.

"Obviously." Arabella dropped the wool as if it had horse muck on it. "Who else would dress like a nun?" She looked sideways at me. "She only gave it to you because I wouldn't have it."

"Oh, shut up," I said. "Can't you say anything kind?"

I let my eyes travel beyond Arabella's sharp chin and the lacy neckline of her dress to the fields and long, rounded hills that were part of Hawkstone, her parents' estate on the Welsh Borders. I'd lived here for seven years, and I don't think Arabella had said one friendly word to me in all that time. It was only after she had left for London and

Court life that I began to truly enjoy my life at Hawkstone – and to finally grow to love the woman I called Aunt Frances, who was Arabella's mother.

Now Arabella had been home for only two weeks yet things had already gone sour between us. In truth I think Aunt Frances dreaded her daughter's visits as much as I did. Arabella hated the country. To her, it was a dull, muddy place full of dull, muddy people and as each day passed that kept her from London and the Queen's Court, her temper grew meaner.

This time I had been daft enough to think that Arabella would be sympathetic because of the predicament I was in. Three weeks before I'd been told that I was to marry a man three times my age, whom I had never met and knew nothing about. And of course, Arabella, who had met him in London, lost no time in telling me how disgusting he was.

The whole matter was a joke to her – a story she would turn into something deeply hilarious so that when she told all her friends at Court, they would clutch their stomachers and laugh.

I tried to ignore the smirk on Arabella's face. "You should count yourself lucky to have a mother who cares for you," I said. "Rather than one who sells you to the highest bidder. I will *not* marry that disgusting old man." My voice cracked and I was furious with myself for showing my feelings.

Arabella shrugged. "No one cares what you want,

Emerald," she said. "You should know that by now. You're fifteen. Lord Suckley needs an heir and your mother needs to get you off her hands. It suits them both."

She jerked her head in the direction of the field of cows we had just passed. "I suggest you spend some time watching that bull over there." She sniggered. "It should broaden your education."

I glared into Arabella's toad-brown eyes. "For one of the Queen's maids, you talk like a bawd," I said. "I am not a cow to be bred from!"

Arabella pushed a few loose strands of her thin, brown hair back under her velvet cap. "Obviously, your mother thinks differently."

I could tell she was pleased with her jibe because she spun round and flounced off down the path before I could reply.

I stopped and watched her make her way down the path towards the grey stone walls of the Hall, her nose in the air and her claret velvet dress swinging in glossy folds from her hips.

I picked up a pebble and knocked off her hat with my first shot.

I was eight when I first came to Hawkstone Hall. My brother, Richard, was fourteen. It was the middle of April and spring had just arrived. The sky was a cold, bright blue and the air full of floating cherry blossom. Two weeks earlier, my father, Stephen, Lord St John, had died. Though he was much older than my mother, it was a terrible shock and completely unexpected. The physicians decided he must have been poisoned from drinking bad water. But our water had always been pure. The only possible explanation was that a sheep had drowned in the stream and tainted it. Two farm boys searched up and down for a waterlogged body, but found nothing – not even a tuft of wool stuck on a twig.

It was a terrible time, but there were more shocks to come.

My father had left particular instructions in his will that if he died suddenly, or in unusual circumstances, Richard and I were to be sent from Croft Amber, our home in Northumberland, to live in Wales and become the wards of Sir Charles Mount and his wife, Lady Frances. At the time, no one, least of all Richard and me, could understand why our father would make such an arrangement. We knew only that Sir Charles had been a close friend of our father's before he was married, and that his home, Hawkstone Hall, was hundreds of miles away – the best part of a week along bad roads and rutted tracks.

When we heard what was to happen, Richard and I were devastated. Even then, it was obvious to both of us that we would be leaving our beloved home for a very long time. Those were bad days and I felt as if I was underwater. I heard people talking to me but their voices sounded strange and distorted and sometimes I saw their lips move but heard no sound come out. The only person who seemed unperturbed by my father's death and the news of this arrangement was my mother.

Our mother, Lady Millicent, had always been a remote and forbidding figure. From our earliest childhood, Richard and I had been looked after by nursemaids, and later by governesses and tutors. We rarely saw either of our parents, except on Sundays when we gathered in the chapel for Mass. My mother's relationship with my father was equally distant. I never saw any fondness pass between them. They barely spoke to one another except about the estate matters they had in common, which were few. Even though Croft Amber belonged to my father's family, it was my mother who ran it, and she was a ruthless woman of business. Hungry cattle were more important than hungry people. So any tenant who did not deliver his share of hay at harvest time was immediately thrown out of his cottage and another family taken on. Lady Millicent didn't care if the man had a sick wife or young children. What mattered was the price of beef at the spring market.

My father turned a blind eye to my mother's cruel regime, preferring to spend his time hunting the wild red deer that still lived in parts of the forest to the north of Croft Amber. It was as if my parents had an unspoken arrangement. She had provided him with an heir and the spare had turned out to be me. Her duty done, they lived their lives separately.

When I think of my father, I remember a man who was kind but weak and rather uneasy around children.

Apart from hunting and fishing, his great interests were reading and gathering flints and arrowheads and he spent many days on his own walking and filling a leather bag with his finds.

Apart from Sunday Mass, we only saw him when we were working at our lessons in the long room at the top of the house. There was a window set into the end gable with a high-backed chair beside it. Sometimes he would come and sit in the chair with his book, and stare out over the miles of empty scrubland. I liked to think that it was our company that made him climb the steep stairs up to the attic. But I knew it was because the window in the gable end faced east and on a fine morning, it gave the best light for him to read his precious volumes of the *Naturalis Historiae*. Sometimes, as he passed behind my bench on his way out, he put his hand on my shoulder. He never said anything to me; but even so, I treasured his touch.

I remember one day my father called me into his writing room. He gave me a leather purse embroidered with his crest. "Keep it safe," he said, "and tell no one. Not even Richard."

I held the purse in my hands. I thought perhaps it was full of his treasured flints. But when I tipped it into my lap, I saw forty gold coins.

"Surely you should look after this for me, Father," I said.

My father shook his head. "This is not part of a dowry, Emerald," he said. "This money is for you alone because one day you will need it. None of us knows what the future holds."

A month later, he was dead.

My mother seemed to be more irritated by my father's death than anything else. Her dressmaker had just delivered a chest of skirts and gowns and sleeves for the spring and summer and she had let me look at them, laid out in her dressing room like treasure in a ship's hold. There were red taffeta petticoats embroidered with gold thread, and ruffled partlets that shone with seed pearls. One yellow gown was so thickly embroidered with roses it was as stiff as a sheaf of parchment.

A day after my father had died, I saw my mother scowling furiously as she ordered her maid to pack the clothes with lavender and put them back in the chest. Then she stamped out of the room and slammed the door behind her. At the time, I didn't understand why she was so angry. Then I realised. My mother cared obsessively about her appearance. Now that she was a widow, she would have to put aside her fine clothes and wear plain black.

My father's funeral was held quickly and quietly. By his wish, there was no procession and no banners proclaiming his rank and coat of arms. He slipped into the ground as quickly as he had slipped out of his life on earth.

During the weeks that followed, no one spoke to us about the strange clause in my father's will that banished us from Croft Amber. Our tutor had been sent away. No fire was lit in the schoolroom, so it was too cold to spend much time at our books. Lucky for us, spring came early that year, and the ground dried out so that it was hard enough to ride on and Richard and I spent our days in the stables or riding on the farm. Often we took a hunk of bread from the pantry and some cheese from the dairy room, ordered our ponies to be saddled, and set off into the same scrubland my father had looked at through our schoolroom window. Most days we didn't return until sunset. But no one asked us where we had been.

Every morning I had a sort of dream. I lay in my bed, sure that the door would open and my mother would come. She would walk quietly into my room with a mug of hot milk and honey and an oatcake for my breakfast. She would sit beside me on the bed and put her arms round me and tell me not to be sad, we would only be visiting Hawkstone Hall for a short time and would be home again before summer was over.

I told Richard about the dream. "Gull-brain," he said, as we sat on our ponies later that morning. "You'll be believing in fairies next." But I heard in his voice that he was as hurt and upset as I was.

I refused to let my dream go. "Even Mother wouldn't let us go without a word of comfort."

We were looking across a bright meadow dotted with yellow and orange cowslips. We had played there as children, running through the flowers and playing games of hide and seek. Beyond, a copse of trees shimmered in a green haze that would become leaves before the end of the week. Through the criss-cross of branches we could see the steep, stone-tiled roof of Croft Amber with its impossibly high, narrow brick chimneys. A jackdaw circled round a chimney pot and settled on top.

I turned and saw Richard chewing his lips as he stared at the flapping bird. I knew what he was thinking. Every spring a pair of jackdaws built their nest on that chimney and the servants lit huge fires piled with dried rosemary to try and smoke them out. Last spring, nothing had worked. Richard eventually killed them with his catapult. They had been brilliant shots and our father had given him a silver shilling and made him promise to do the same the next year.

Neither of us spoke as we watched two jackdaws settle confidently on the chimney pot, each with a beakful of twigs.

"Richard—" I started at last, wanting him to stop the thoughts that were making my head hurt.

"Shut up," he said harshly, and kicked his pony into a gallop.

On the morning we left Croft Amber for ever, the sky stayed as dark as a bruise and the heavy rain that had begun at dawn did not let up.

That morning I had woken in the dark. I still couldn't believe I was leaving the house I had been born in.

The carriage that was to take us part of the way to

Wales looked shabby and uncared for as it waited in the rain on the cobbled yard beyond the front porch.

Our coachman opened the creaking leather door and we climbed inside. The walls were covered in mouldy blotches and the leather seats sprouted tufts of damp, itchy horsehair, and there was dirty straw on the floor. It was like crawling into an animal's den.

Whether it was because of the rain – my mother had a terror of catching a chill – or because she simply couldn't be bothered, my mother didn't come out with us to the carriage. Her last words to us were spoken from the shelter of the gabled porch. "Run, else you'll soak yourselves."

As the coachman slammed the door shut and clambered up on to his seat, I could see my mother's raised hand, but she was already turning back.

The coach lurched forward. When I looked again, the door to the house was closed and my mother had gone.

Richard put his arm awkwardly round my shoulder. "We don't need her," he said, in a voice that sounded as if it was going to crack. "I'll look after you."

The coach rattled over the cobblestones and out through the gates of the lodge.

I never saw Croft Amber again.

Shortly after we arrived at Hawkstone Hall, Richard went away to sea. My heart broke when he left, even though I knew he had to go. We had been so close after our father's death but at Hawkstone we just seemed to make each other miserable. There was a life for me in Wales but nothing for Richard. His love was the sea.

My father had left him a small amount of money for his keep so when a certain Captain Maxwell asked him join the ship's company on *The Pigeon,* Richard left immediately. Soon he stopped writing letters and I rarely heard from him. It was as if he wanted to turn his back on our life at Croft Amber even if it meant turning his back on me too.

A year after that, the man I had come to call Uncle Charles told me that Croft Amber had been sold to settle family debts, and that my mother had married a powerful Catholic lord called Henry of Orgon. I had never felt so alone. First my father, then my home – and Richard far away, somewhere off the coast of South America. It seemed as though I had no one left in the world. But that night Arabella's mother, Lady Frances, came to my room and took me in her arms and comforted me while I grieved for everything I had lost. From then on, she became the mother I had never known.

Seven years passed. During all that time, I never heard once from my mother, until a letter arrived addressed to my Uncle Charles. She was writing to inform Sir Charles that her daughter, Emerald, was to be married to a nobleman called Lord Edmund Suckley and asked that Lord Suckley be welcomed at Hawkstone Hall. My mother said it was Lord Suckley's wish to satisfy a natural curiosity concerning the character and person of his future wife, since there was no likeness in the form of a portrait or ink drawing available.

The day after my mother's letter arrived, Uncle Charles summoned me to the little room above the courtyard where he kept the household record books. There he told me that since I had very little in terms of a dowry, Lord Suckley was a worthy match and I should accept my mother's proposal with good grace.

I thought of the forty gold coins my father had given me and decided to keep them secret. They were all I had in the world and I was not going to hand them over to a man I already hated.

So it was arranged that when the roads dried up, Lord Suckley would come to look me over. It was as if I was some kind of breeding animal. Just as Arabella had said.

I must have been walking in a sort of daze since I'd spoken to Arabella because when I looked up I was almost on the bank of the narrow river that ran through a cut in the land, a good three fields away from the farm.

I sat down and leaned back against an oak tree. It was sheltered here and, even though it was barely mid-morning, I could feel the heat of the spring sun on my cheeks. The ground was stony and I was glad of the thick wool skirt that Aunt Frances had given me. I picked up a pebble and aimed it at a magpie perched on a branch on the other side of the river. I missed, but there was a squawk and the branch bounced as the bird flew away.

I thought about magpies and how they snatched baby birds from their nests. It was Aunt Frances who had taught me to recognise their harsh cry. She always had a pebble in her pocket for a magpie, and had taught me to carry one, too.

It was also Aunt Frances who had given me the skills a mother should teach her daughter: how to grow herbs and dry them; how to make potions and tinctures that healed and soothed – liquorice and comfrey for colds in the lung, mint and balm leaf for stomach upsets. I could fix a leech on to a man's vein without fainting at the blood and tie a splint to straighten a shattered bone. Aunt Frances had taught me how to sew and weave and play the simplest tunes on a lute, but not how to dance or play cards or paint my chin to hide spots.

Arabella floated into my mind, as she always did when I thought of her mother. They were not in the least alike, and their differences seemed to grow stronger as time went on.

Aunt Frances was tall, with even features in a long face, and her eyes were the blue of spring violets. Her wavy hair had been dark gold, but was now white. It was still thick and sometimes, when I brushed it out in her bedroom, I thought it was the most beautiful part of her.

By contrast Arabella was short, and everything about

her was angular. Her thin hair never grew thick and lustrous, even though she rarely washed it and only rinsed it in rainwater.

Where her mother was generous in all of her dealings, Arabella kept a tally of what she was owed. It was as if she had an abacus in her head. She moved her favours to and fro like wooden beads to use them to her best advantage.

"I thought I'd find you here." Aunt Frances interrupted my thoughts. She stood in front of me, carrying a basket of nettles. "What did you say to Arabella? She has a face like a basin full of worms."

I stared at the nettles, then at my aunt's face. She wasn't smiling, and I found myself lost for words. Surely she of all people could guess at the kind of conversation I'd just had with Arabella? But I didn't want another argument. Particularly with her.

"I'll help you pick nettles," I said. "I can put them in my apron."

Aunt Frances sighed. "You must give up behaving like a child, Emerald," she said.

I heard the gurgling of the river and a harsh squawking on the far bank, as if the magpie had come back to mock me. If I couldn't speak the truth to my aunt, then I was truly alone in this nightmare.

I said, "I would rather eat maggots than have that man Suckley touch me."

"Your mother has given her agreement," replied Aunt Frances.

"I am not a breeding animal!" I shouted, losing my temper like I'd hoped not to. "You know as well as I do that my mother can't force a marriage on me without Richard's permission."

"Don't take us for fools, Emerald," replied Aunt Frances. Her face reddened. "We don't want this marriage any more than you do. But Richard is at sea. No one knows when he'll be back and . . ." She turned away.

"And *what*?" I demanded. "I should be grateful for a secure future? You get the poor, penniless ward off your hands?"

"Stop it, Emerald," cried my aunt. She tried to look at me, but her eyes slid away. "The truth is that your mother would make a dangerous enemy to all of us, even Richard. And the sooner you know that, the better it will be for everyone."

It was as if she had thrown a bucket of cold water in my face.

"You owe my mother nothing!" I blurted. But the look in her eyes told me I was wrong.

Through the trees, the timber-framed gables of the Hall seemed to float on a cloud of pink and white blossom, and the white lime-washed plaster sparkled in the sun.

Earlier that day, I had thought how beautiful it was. But now it was blotted out by the question that turned in my head like a thick, black snake. How could my mother be an enemy to the people who had taken me in?

"I came to tell you that Lord Suckley arrives before nightfall," said Aunt Frances in a dull voice.

My mouth opened and shut, but nothing came out. No one had expected him for another week.

Through the top of a tree, I saw the unmistakable shape of Arabella in a window on the second floor of the house. Now I understood why she had suddenly arrived in the orchard that morning. I should have guessed there was a reason because Arabella never usually left her bed until noon. She'd been sent down to talk some sense into me.

Aunt Frances had betrayed me, just like my mother. I hated them both.

"I'm glad of Lord Suckley's visit," I said, in the nastiest voice I could manage. "He will be company for Arabella. She's already told me he is too gouty to dance and too stupid for cards."

"Emerald," snapped Aunt Frances. "For your own sake—"

"No," I shouted back and my voice broke. "For *your* sake, Aunt. I will act my part. No more."

I walked away so she couldn't see that my hands were shaking.

Chapter Two

When my head starts to ache with things I don't understand, I take myself off fishing. I'm good at catching fish and by the time I close my wicker basket there are usually half a dozen slippery bodies inside. Best of all, I've had a chance to think, and that always means my head doesn't hurt as much.

Now all I wanted was to fetch my rod and basket without being seen and get down to the river on my own. So, after I left Aunt Frances, I doubled back through the orchard and over the gate into the walled vegetable garden.

Apart from a few rows of leeks and a patch of spring cabbages, there was nothing much growing. It was still cold and too early to sow but I knew that would all change as the weather warmed up. The vegetable garden was my aunt's kingdom; the soil was always dug to the fineness of breadcrumbs and everything she planted flourished.

Even the pear and plum trees she had trained along the high brick walls produced baskets and baskets of fruit. Last year I picked our first white peaches and packed them in stone jars filled with sugar and brandy and gave them out over Christmas. Their sweetness was the talk of the village.

At the far end of the garden, an arch led into a small flagstone courtyard beyond the kitchen door. I hid behind the wall and peered round the corner. Sarah was sitting on a wooden stool outside the back door, gutting plucked hens. Sarah was a couple of years older than me and she had come to Hawkstone as an orphan. Her parents had been distant relations of my Uncle Charles and had lost their lives and everything they owned when their farm burned to the ground in Somerset. Sarah had come to the Hall to join the steward's service on the estate. Aunt Frances had been keen that I had a friend and so Sarah and I had played together as children and sometimes we learned our lessons together. She was a tall girl with thoughtful eyes and an eagle's beak of a nose, but the best thing about Sarah was that you knew you could always rely on her. If Sarah made a promise, she kept it.

Then the steward's wife died of the mumps and at the same time the kitchen maid went down with the coughing sickness. The next thing I knew there was no time to play with Sarah any more and she stopped calling me by my first name.

Sarah looked up when she saw me. "If you're off fishing," she said, wrinkling her nose at the stink of the hens' innards, "Cook'd be pleased to have a few grayling. There's guests and you're eating in the Great Chamber tonight." She pulled out something green and lumpy from inside a hen's body, and slapped it down in a bucket. "Yech! These are best fit for a hog."

"Then they will do nicely for a certain Lord Suckley," I said, knowing full well that everyone in the house knew my business. "Arabella tells me he is just like one." I knew I was being childish but it made me feel better. Sarah wiped her nose with her hand, smearing it with sticky blood. She gave me a steady look. "So it's him you're to marry."

"I have not agreed to marry anyone, Sarah," I said, as calmly as I could manage. "And you would be doing me a service if you said as much to Cook."

"I'll do more than that." Sarah pointed to the green-flecked gobbets in the bucket. "I'm serving tonight. I'll give Suckley a special plate. There's a hen that fair stinks out the back and I'll smear it with gut gripe to be sure." She smiled at me because she knew I was upset. "A night in the jakes should damp him down a bit."

I laughed out loud. I hadn't heard anyone talk about gut gripe for a long time. It was made of chicken droppings mixed up with rotten crayfish. When we were children, Sarah and I used to pretend we had given it to our enemies and laugh ourselves silly as we imagined the consequences. "For that I'll bring you back six graylings and a prize," I said.

21

Sarah dropped the last carcass into the bucket and grinned at me.

"It's a bargain," she said.

Two hours later half a dozen grayling, each one the length of my foot, lay on the grass beside me. I liked fishing for grayling. I had taught myself how to cast and to make the lure dance on the water like a paddling bug. I always caught a fish.

I tied on a fly I had made that winter. Making flies was something to do during the long nights and always made me feel as if I was back on the river. I used odd lengths of coloured silk thread from my embroidery box. Each fly was tied differently and I named them after the stars I had learned about as a child. As I cast my line out over the water, I imagined the fly as a star soaring through the universe. It was a trick my father had taught me: *"If you put your thoughts where the fish can't hear them, they won't know you're there."*

I cast for the last time and watched as the loops of line flew across the river. It was a perfect cast but, this time, I didn't feel the quick tug of a grayling. As I pulled in, it felt as if the fly was caught on a rotten log. Then coils of line disappeared into the water. A second later another tug nearly jerked the rod from my hand and I saw a huge pike zigzag across the river towards a patch of dark water under the bank.

For the next hour, I played the pike and I followed my

father's advice. I thought of nothing but Lord Suckley. Somehow I needed to distract him while I waited for Richard to come back and put a stop to this dreadful marriage. As for my mother, the less I knew about what kind of enemy she was to my aunt and uncle, the better. I'd got on very well without her for a long time and from past experience, she only caused hurt. Even so, finding a way to keep Suckley at arm's length was going to be very difficult.

I knew a lot about fish but not much about men and their ways.

Arabella had once told me about a courtier who had fixed a mirror to his cuff so he could cheat at cards when he played with the Queen.

I didn't understand. "But surely the Queen prefers skilled players?"

Arabella rolled her eyes. "Dull wit," she said. "The mirror made sure the Queen always won."

I still didn't understand.

"Because the Queen *wants* to win," explained Arabella, as if she was talking to a simpleton. "If you're a Queen, you get what you want, no matter how." She burst into nasty laughter. "You wouldn't last five minutes in London."

I pulled back my rod and all thoughts of Arabella and Suckley disappeared. It was time to land my pike.

Normally you need a net to land a pike. You slide the net under the fish while it's in shallow water and yank it up before it has time to wriggle free. All I had was my apron and a bit of a plan.

I stepped over to a spit of stones in the shallow water. Then I bent down and laid my apron in the water, weighting it with stones but leaving the ties on either side floating free, while I kept the line tight on the pike. My plan was to pull in the pike until it was over the apron, then yank up the ties and trap it in the rough cloth.

The huge fish was barely six feet away from me now. Very gently, I drew it over the apron.

I made myself imagine Lord Suckley's face. I saw bristles poking out of a lumpy, red-veined nose. I saw black stubs where teeth had once been and smelled the stink of rotten gums. His lips were wet and rubbery like two pink slugs pressed together. I brought his face towards me so it got bigger and bigger and the spittle on his lips was almost on my neck…

I yanked up the ties and heaved the fish ashore with such a hard jerk, I fell backwards head over heels. But when I got up the fish was there on the edge of the river, green and shining and huge as a monster.

"Bravo!" A skinny girl with red hair skipped from side to side on the riverbank. "Bravo!"

"Meg Catchpole!" I cried. I was so pleased with myself I felt a huge grin spreading over my face. "How long have you been watching me?"

"Long enough to tell thems in the kitchen," replied Meg, her eyes bright as candles. "I'd never have believed it if I ain't seen it meself!"

"And I never thought I would do it!" It was almost

impossible not to whoop with delight. I knotted the apron ties tight round the heavy, thrashing fish and threw it as hard as I could up the bank.

Meg waited until I was sitting on the grass beside her, and then pushed her freckly face into mine. "Is it true what they's saying, Miss Em?" she asked, prodding the pike with her foot. "Is it true you are to marry a fat-kidneyed lordy lord?"

I gave her a shove so she tumbled sideways. "No, it's not true and it's none of your business, you nosy baggage! And stop poking my pike with your boot."

"A jumped-up maggoty ape, that's what they're saying."

"Shut your mouth, young Meg," I said, pulling open the apron ties and seeing my prize close up for the first time.

It was a big pike and it thrashed on the ground, gasping for air. Rows of curved teeth glinted in its ugly, overshot jaw, and I knew it would have a finger off me if I got too near.

"A maggoty ape! A maggoty ape!" cried Meg, dancing about as I took my knife from my belt.

"For heaven's sake, hold your tongue!" I wrapped the apron round one hand to hold the fish still. "If anyone hears your nonsense, you'll get a belting."

"Why should I?" said Meg. "That's what the master called him."

I put the tip of the knife on the back of the pike's head and pushed down hard. There was a *crunch* of bone and

25

gristle; then it twisted once and lay still on the grass. I turned back to Meg. "You mustn't make up stories."

"They're not stories!" cried Meg. "I was under the table in the hall. I heard everything."

My stomach turned over. "What do you mean, you heard everything?" Already the pike's shiny, silver scales were going dull and its eyes had turned cloudy. It wasn't a shiny, green prize any more, just a dead fish. I began to wish I'd never caught it.

"I hides there, Miss Emerald," said Meg, her shoulders sagging at the tone of my voice. "Ever since that Turkey rug got put over the top, it's safe as a cave underneath." She pulled at my skirt. "I swear by my dead ma's grave, miss. The master called your lordy lord a pox-marked ape. Said he was an oaf with no breeding."

A magpie screeched on the other side of the bank, but I was in no mood to throw stones. Uncle Charles had told me that Suckley was a good match.

My head was ringing.

Why had he lied to me?

I pulled the knife from the dead fish and wiped the slimy mess of blood and silver scales off on to the grass. "When did you hear this?" I asked Meg.

"Before breakfast today," said Meg eagerly. She was clearly pleased I believed her now. "Cook was baking pies so I went to the kitchen to take one but then I couldn't because Hetty was there and she don't like me. Says I'm worse than a weasel."

"Never mind what Hetty says," I said. "What happened then?"

"I had to go out down the corridor and through the front hall, didn't I?" said Meg. "No one was about so I thought I'd risk a beating. So there I was almost halfway across when I hears 'em on the stairs and I hides under the table. They was arguin', miss," she said. "The master was angry with her ladyship."

I frowned, not wanting to believe her. In all of my years at Hawkstone, I had never heard my uncle raise his voice to his wife. As for arguments between them, there weren't any.

"What were they saying?"

"Sir Charles said," – Meg put on a deep voice – "*We took an oath, Frances, we can't break it.*"

Meg's voice went high, imitating my aunt. "*Our oath was to the girl's father, not to Millicent, my lord.*"

I stared at her. "Are you sure that was the name her ladyship said?"

"Sure as eggs, Miss Emerald," said Meg. "Who's Millicent?"

"My mother."

Meg stared at me. "I don't understand."

"Neither do I," I said.

"Anyway, they began to quarrel," said Meg. "I've never heard such fierce words. Mistress says an oath that's been broken ain't binding no more. Master says it's no business of hers, and mistress spits like a cat, and says it was his

27

idea in the first place. Then mistress called for Hetty to fetch Arabella to her bedroom."

I thought back to that morning and remembered that when I'd met Arabella outside her mother's room, she had instantly asked me to come walking. I recalled Aunt Frances' words to me when we met in the orchard. *"What did you say to Arabella? She has a face like a basin full of worms."* Now I was sure she had asked Arabella to talk me into obeying my mother's wishes. But why would she do that if she didn't feel bound to obey them herself? And what was this about an oath? I realised that I couldn't put my head in the sand any more. If I was going to stop my mother forcing this marriage on me, I had to find out what was between her and my guardians.

I rubbed my hands over my face. They were sticky with fish blood, but I didn't care.

"Don't fret yourself, miss," said Meg stoutly. "I knows every hiding place. I'll get your answers for you." She folded her skinny arms and stuck out her chin. "Me and Sarah ain't having you go off with no maggoty ape." She gulped and a tear dribbled down her cheek. "They's never goin' to make you marry 'im, neither."

"They're going to try, Meg." I wiped her tear away and made myself smile to cheer her up. "But don't you worry, I ain't having none of it, either." I wrapped up the pike in my apron. "Take this to Cook and tell her I caught it specially for Lord Suckley."

"What?"

"Hush, Meg," I said. "Just because I say it, doesn't follow that I *mean* it."

Meg's eyes slid over to the basket full of grayling. "And the fish?" she asked slyly.

"For you and Sarah," I replied. "Spies' wages. Now go."

Meg stared at me. "Ain't you coming?"

I shook my head. "I haven't seen Molly today." I ruffled Meg's hair. "I'd rather go on my own."

"I understands, miss," said Meg, and she ran off lugging the basket of fish with the pike in the apron under her arm.

Molly was my bear. I had raised her from a cub. Richard had brought her from London a few years after he had joined his ship. She'd been wrapped in an old coat and packed into a wooden box sucking warm milk from a cloth.

Richard had won Molly at a gambling club in Southwark, near the bear-baiting pits at Paris Garden. The story went that after the mayor's mastiffs had ripped the guts out of a female bear, the bear-keeper had found her tiny cub hidden in the filthy straw of the stall and sold it to the first person he saw wearing a decent doublet, who turned out to be a gambler called Weems. When Richard sat down at the card table, Weems had just lost his last sovereign, so he bet the cub instead.

Richard told me he had originally intended to throw the cub into the river, since it had no chance of surviving without a mother. Then he had remembered that Briar, my deerhound, had just had a litter, so she might accept the cub to suckle. Since he was coming to Wales the next day, he had decided to give the tiny cub a chance.

I say I raised Molly. Actually, it was Tom Bounds who kept her alive. Tom was the stable man, and if anyone could save an animal's life, he could. To this day, I can see myself standing by Tom's side as he took the half-dead cub from the box and held her amongst the squirming litter of puppies, talking to Briar and stroking her head, until she let the bear cub find a teat and suck.

"I ain't makin' no promises, Miss Emerald," Tom had said as he stood up in the gloom of the straw-filled stable box. "Hound might change her mind and that will be that."

But Briar didn't change her mind. Soon I could feed Molly milk through a reed. A few weeks later she was taking sops and vegetables from my hand. Now she was as heavy as a newborn calf and the smell of her was as strong as musk.

I ran over the cobbled yard in front of the stables and went in. There was a barrel of apples beside the door and I put a couple in my pocket. Inside the stables it was warm and murky and smelled of horse dung and straw. The horses shuffled in their places and some of them whinnied and rattled their bridles as I went past them. Molly's pen was built on at the far end with its own door.

I lifted the bar on the door and opened it. The sharp smell of bear made my nostrils tingle and I almost sneezed.

I called out Molly's name like I always did and sat down on the three-legged stool in the corner. I took out the apples and called her again. It was like a game. The second time she heard her name, Molly stood up in the straw and snuffed at me. Then she waddled over and put her huge head in my lap. When I'd rubbed her ears and patted the thick fur on her neck, I held out the apples and she sat down on her haunches to eat.

"Good girl, Molly," I said.

She swallowed both apples at once and looked at me expectantly. I hadn't taken her out for two days and I knew she could smell the spring air. I sat on the stool and she leaned against me like she always did, waiting for me to tie a rope to the chain around her neck and take her out past the horses and into the sunshine.

I patted her head and smoothed the fur round her eyes. "I can't take you out today, Molly," I told her. "Something bad's happened."

Molly snuffled and licked my hand with her long, rough tongue. "If you were me, you'd understand," I said.

She stared up at me reproachfully then grunted and lay down in the straw at my feet.

I looked at the big, furry animal I'd known since she had been small enough to fit in my shoe. Molly was my dearest thing. If I was made to marry Lord Suckley, I would have to leave her behind. I bent down and whispered into her ears. "I'll find a way out, little one," I promised. "No maggoty ape will take me away from you."

Molly put her snout between her paws, sighed deeply and closed her eyes. It was as if she didn't have to worry any more because she trusted everything I said.

I stood up and closed her door behind me.

As I walked back to the Hall, I saw a bull climb clumsily on to the back of a cow in the field Arabella had pointed at. He was roaring and snorting and his mouth was foaming with spit. I found myself staring under his belly and thinking about what Arabella had said about broadening my education. What I saw disgusted me and, if I'm honest, even frightened me a little.

Suddenly I felt a rage that practically lifted me off the ground. Arabella had done me a favour. If Suckley tried to touch me, I'd stab him with my pocket knife.

Chapter Three

Sarah found me in the back hall where I was trying to sneak past the dry larder and up the stairs to the first floor.

"His lordship arrived early," she said. "Mistress has been looking for you everywhere! You're to go to her dressing room straight away."

"Does she seem angry?"

"No, but you're to have a bath." She grinned. "So you won't smell of bear."

I was just about to reply when Arabella's crowing laughter floated through an open window. "Come now, Lord Suckley, enough of my chicken-pen chatter. What news do you bring from London?"

I held my breath, hoping to hear the voice that would reply. But there was only the *crash* of a pewter tray being set down on a table, then the *bang* of a door slamming shut.

"You'll hear him soon enough," said Sarah, reading my mind. "He's been giving out orders ever since he came through the gates."

We ran up the narrow stairs and along the passageway

to my room. Sarah opened the door and pulled me inside. "Now get in that bath, else I'll be in trouble."

A wooden bathtub, lined with thick linen sheets to protect against splinters and help keep in the water, had been dragged into the middle of the room. Beside it stood six buckets, steam rising in curls from their lids. As Sarah dragged each one up the side and splashed the water into the tub, I undressed and waited until the bath was ready. It felt good to be out of my clothes and I wasn't shy in front of Sarah. We knew each other too well. But as I looked down at my full breasts and below to the black, curly hair that covered my sex, I tried to imagine being naked with a man and I couldn't. Then I thought of the bull in the field and I couldn't stop a shiver going through me. Without thinking, I reached for a shawl to cover myself.

"Quick, before it gets cold," said Sarah.

If she'd seen the look on my face, she said nothing. She scooped up a handful of dried geranium leaves and the room filled with their scent.

I let the shawl drop and climbed into the bath.

"Hot enough?" asked Sarah. Without waiting for a reply, she tipped a pitcher of water over my bare shoulders, rubbed a cake of our own soap on to a rough cloth and began to scrub my back. "She was right."

"Who was right?" I blinked the water out of my eyes.

"Mistress was." Sarah wrung out the cloth and began to drag a wooden comb through my hair. "You *stink* of bear."

"But I've hardly touched Molly today," I protested.

34

Sarah pulled a face. "Miss Emerald, you *always* smell of bear."

"In that case, let me out before you wash it all off."

Sarah held up the pitcher. I splashed her with water and she poured the pitcher over my head. Just then, Hetty walked into the room with Aunt Frances' clothes over her arm and the happy mood in the room disappeared.

She sniffed and frowned at Sarah, not even looking at me. "Her ladyship says I'm not to dress her in these if she stinks."

I stepped out of the bath, yanked the clothes from Hetty's arms and dumped them on the floor. "How dare you speak of me like that?" I snapped. Hetty was my aunt's maid and I was sure it was her chatter that had started the whole house talking.

"Get out, you blabbing baggage," I shouted, wrapping myself in a sheet. "How I smell is none of your business. Sarah will dress me."

"*Sarah*? But she's a kitchen girl!" Hetty's eyes bulged in her spiteful face as she picked the clothes off the floor and laid them out on the bed. But before she could say one more word, I shoved her through the open door.

Sarah didn't speak as she sloshed the grimy bathwater into leather buckets and set them against the wall. But now the silence between us was a bond. And I felt almost grateful to Hetty for getting me more time with Sarah.

We both stared at the clothes draped over the bed. There were fine linen smocks and petticoats as well as silk dresses and gowns and pairs of sleeves made of thickly embroidered taffeta. They were the most beautiful clothes I had ever seen and it looked as if Aunt Frances had never worn them.

Sarah held out a smock and a pair of silk stockings. Until then I had always knitted my own out of wool. As I tied the ribbon under my knees, it felt as if my legs were wrapped in gossamer. Then I stood, still as a child, as Sarah laced me into a canvas bodice stiffened with whalebone and held my hand as I stepped into a hooped petticoat.

"There now," said Sarah, hauling on the ties that criss-crossed up my back until I could hardly breathe. "That's the easy bit over with. Now you have to make a plan."

We stared at the velvets and silks and taffetas on the bed. "What do you want him to think when he first sees you?"

I didn't reply at first, even though I'd spent most of the morning thinking about little else. "I want him to see an innocent," I said at last. "Then it will be easier to play for time."

Sarah nodded as if she approved. "Leave it to me," she said. "No looking in the mirror until I'm finished with you."

I grinned. It was as if we were starting off on a new adventure together after years of being apart.

For the next half hour, I gazed out over the roofs of the Hall and only moved when Sarah told me to. And as she fitted and tugged and buttoned, I told her how I was going to play Suckley like a fish to keep him at bay until Richard came back.

"That could be months away," said Sarah. "Suckley won't wait for ever, especially if your mother's keen to see the match."

I pulled a face. "I can't write to Richard before I've laid eyes on the wretch."

Sarah pinned my hair up under a plain cap sewn with pearls and pulled down a couple of tendrils on either side of my face.

"There's only one that knows tricks around men," said Sarah. "And that's Arabella."

"Arabella won't help me. There's nothing in it for her."

"There's her own entertainment," replied Sarah. "It's always the way with her sort. It would be more amusing for her to watch Suckley try and keep his dignity while you play him for a fool than see you being forced into marrying him." She turned me towards the mirror. "What do you think?"

I found myself staring at someone I hardly recognised. For the first time, I realised that my high cheekbones gave my face shape and that my nose, which I'd always thought of as too long and bumpy, was the perfect size above my mouth, which was large and full-lipped.

The colours Sarah had chosen for me to wear made me look sweet and eager to please. I wore a bodice made of pale green silk and my peach velvet skirt fell from my hips in soft folds. The gown was cut from cream satin and embroidered down the front with violets. As a last touch, Sarah had fixed a collar of French lace over my breasts, which gave me a fetching air of modesty while drawing attention to my throat and neck.

I looked like a different person. The girl in the mirror would have fainted at the whiff of a bear and she had certainly never climbed a tree or gutted a fish in her life.

I dragged my eyes away from the mirror and turned to Sarah in astonishment. "Where did you learn how to do this?" I asked.

"My mother taught me," replied Sarah, looking pleased. "We made the clothes ourselves and I practised on dolls." She shook out a pair of sleeves and put them back on the bed. "When I came here, I was to train to be Lady Frances' maid but the steward's wife died before she could arrange it and somehow I was given work in the kitchen."

I frowned. How could I have not known any of this?

"I never told you," said Sarah, as if she knew what I was thinking. "I didn't want to get you involved."

Someone was calling for hot water in the corridor. Sarah looked across at the row of leather buckets by the door. "I must go."

"Wait." I took her arm and held it. "Would you dress me again?"

Sarah hugged me. "Of course."

"You look the image of your grandmother St John," said the voice of Aunt Frances.

Sarah and I sprang apart. Hetty must have left the door ajar because neither of us had heard my aunt come into the room.

Sarah grabbed an armful of wet sheets, bobbed and left.

"I don't know why I never noticed before," continued Aunt Frances as the door shut behind her. "You are taller, of course, but otherwise…" Her voice fell away and she shook her head. "It's remarkable."

"You never told me you knew my father's family." I was trying to keep any sharpness out of my voice. The last thing I wanted was another argument.

"No, perhaps I didn't." Aunt Frances shrugged. "Your father's mother was a lady-in-waiting in Queen Anne's court in the old king's time. Her name was Eleanor and when I was a young girl, she was very kind to me."

I stared at her. "How long did you live at Court?"

"Not long," replied Aunt Frances. "A few months. I hated it."

"Why didn't you tell me about my grandmother before?"

Aunt Frances looked away. "I suppose I thought it would upset you after the death of your father, and then the years passed and it didn't seem to matter any more." She paused. "Eleanor died before you were born."

"My father never mentioned her either," I said half to myself. "I would have liked to have known about her."

My aunt put a wooden box in my hands. "Eleanor left

39

me these," she said as if she hadn't heard me. "She would have wanted you to have them."

I opened the box. Two beautiful pendant earrings lay cushioned in red velvet. Each one was made up of three emeralds surrounded by diamonds. I held them up and watched the light from the window sparkle through the stones.

"Did she have green eyes too?"

Aunt Frances nodded as if she was seeing a face in her mind. "Yes, she was as beautiful as you."

No one had ever called me beautiful before. It made me feel awkward and oddly tongue-tied. I put on the earrings and made a deep curtsey. "Your clothes would make anyone beautiful, Aunt."

But all the time I was thinking how strange it was that she would chose this moment to tell me I was beautiful when she knew Suckley was waiting downstairs to ogle me as soon as I walked into the room. The words tumbled out of my mouth before I could stop myself. "I hope my grandmother wasn't made to marry a loathsome old man twice her age."

My aunt stepped back as if I had slapped her. "Take care not to be rude this evening," she said in her coldest voice.

When we were children, Richard and I used to play a game. There were never many visitors to Croft Amber, but when they did come, we were always sent up to the schoolroom. We used to hide where we could hear the visitors, even if we couldn't see them. In our game, whenever I heard a voice, I had to describe the face of the person I thought matched the voice, and Richard would sketch it. He was quick with his pencil and very soon a likeness would appear on his paper.

As our parents led their guests up the main stairs to the big chamber on the first floor, we would race up the back stairs to the attic that ran the length of the house. At one end there was a gap in the oak boards that gave a view of the space in front of the fireplace. We crouched over the gap, waiting until the guests had warmed their backs against the fire. When we could see their faces, we compared them to the drawings and Richard gave me marks out of ten for accuracy. I never got less than nine.

Now, as I stood at the top of the curving oak staircase leading down to the hall, I heard two unfamiliar voices. The first was deep, with a French accent. There was laughter and as I listened to the rise and fall of the conversation, a face gradually took shape in my mind. I guessed he was a tall man with a long face, perhaps forty, or older. His voice spoke of caution, and I imagined him being as surefooted as a panther. The second voice was squeaky but harsh at the same time. It was unpleasant to listen to, and the face I imagined was just as unpleasant – saggy and bad-tempered.

I was sure it was the voice of Lord Suckley.

"Three days of rutted tracks since Macclesfield," said Suckley, his voice rising petulantly as he spoke. "The mare needs new shoes and my arse still aches from the saddle."

There was a short silence then my uncle spoke. "A speedy journey, my Lord Suckley," he said as if he hadn't heard the complaint. "I can assure you I have known worse." His voice was light and dismissive but, for someone who had called his guest an ape with no manners, Uncle Charles sounded remarkably restrained. Once again I asked myself what hold my mother could possibly have over him.

There was the sound of a tankard of ale being set down heavily. "Where is the wench?" demanded Suckley.

"I beg your pardon, my lord?" Uncle Charles' voice turned thin and I could hear that his restraint was cracking, and felt grateful. "Do you speak of my ward?"

"Have done with your stiff talk, sir," replied Suckley rudely. "Wench or ward, no matter. I am here to claim Emerald St John as my wife."

There was a silence and I could feel my uncle's anger. It was the Frenchman who spoke first.

"I beg you, Sir Charles," he said. "Please excuse my friend. He is tired. We made few stops on our journey."

"Hardly a decent inn to stop *at*," muttered Lord Suckley.

I heard the Frenchman's uneasy laughter. "Always so frank, my lord," he said smoothly. The voice changed. "An admirable quality. Wouldn't you agree, Sir Charles?"

My uncle didn't answer and I could still feel his anger.

It was time for me to join them.

I made my way down the stairs. As I turned the corner and walked into the hall, the three men stepped back. There was my uncle. Beside him, nearest the fire, was an older man with a barrel-shaped chest and skinny legs. He had a face like a pig with the greedy eyes of a weasel. It could only be Lord Suckley and the thought of his hands coming anywhere near me made me want to throw up.

I looked at the third man. His rich, accented voice had completely deceived me. This man was slight and blond with a face like a cherub and eyes so pale that they were almost colourless. An uneasy feeling prickled in my mind. Richard would have shrugged, and told me I couldn't be right all the time, but I knew my mistake was a warning. Something about this man was dangerous.

I walked across the oak boards of the hall. Clean rushes had been laid and smelled faintly of sweet hay. I made myself smile at Lord Suckley.

His eyes glittered, and he began to make a curious grunting noise under his breath – I doubt he was even aware of it. I let my eyelashes drop and made myself blush by imagining him standing in a puddle with his brecches round his knees.

"Emerald!" said my uncle as he strode towards me. "You look magnificent!"

"Fine clothes, Uncle," I said. I touched my earrings and smiled. "And my grandmother's jewels."

My uncle frowned for moment then he said awkwardly,

"They suit you well." I held his eyes and I understood that he would have preferred it if my aunt had given them to Arabella.

"Come," he said. "Let me introduce you to our guest."

Close up, Lord Suckley was positively disgusting. He had a wart the size of a raisin on his left nostril and his eyes were watery in their pouches of wrinkles. As I made a deep curtsey in front of him, I promised myself that I would drink poison rather than marry this man.

"Lord Suckley. " I drew myself up to my full height and looked down at his thin, greasy hair. "I am honoured by your visit. Arabella has told me much about you."

"All to my credit, I trust." Suckley's wet mouth broke into a leering smile that showed the blackened stubs of his front teeth. "Because you and I must become acquainted."

Before I could stop him, he had grabbed my hand and brought it to his lips.

I was too shocked to hide my surprise. I pulled my hand back, feeling my fingers sticky with his spit and recovered myself.

"A friendship cannot be hurried, my lord," I murmured, trying to smile. "We will have time enough to become acquainted over the next few days."

My words were wasted on him.

"I am not pledged to become your friend, my lady," he said with a snarl. "You will be my wife before the summer is out."

44

His rudeness rang through the room like a cracked bell. For a second we stood awkwardly, like players who had forgotten their lines. No one, not even the baby-faced Frenchman, could think of anything to say.

Then Arabella swept into the room. She took in the situation in an instant and cried, "Well met, my lord! Tell me again, which roads were most rutted? Which was the dirtiest inn?"

I watched in something akin to awe as Arabella slipped her hand through Suckley's arm and drew him towards the warmth of the fire, laughing as she tapped his doublet with her ringed forefinger. "Faith, your heart must be truly lost to endure such misery!" As she turned to pick up a goblet of wine from a servant, she caught my eye and winked.

I couldn't understand why she was being so helpful, then I remembered what Sarah had said. She was right. For Arabella, making a fool out of an old goat like Suckley was much better sport than poking fun at a simpleton like me.

"Pray, madam, may I introduce myself?"

The man with the baby face made me an elaborate bow. There was something horrible about such a deep voice coming from those cherubic lips. Despite the heat from the fire, I shivered.

"I am Pierre Marchand. My family are perfumiers and serve the Comte Landemer in Normandy."

I made no move to reply. He looked sideways at me as

if he understood that I was unused to company and too tongue-tied to respond.

"You may ask yourself what business a French perfumier has with so distinguished a lord, and I will tell you. While I am a perfumier by profession, the healing power of herbs is my study. When I heard from Comte Landemer that his old friend was coming to Hawkstone Hall to meet his bride, I put myself forward as his travelling companion. I was eager to meet your guardian, you see. Lady Frances' skills are spoken of all over my country."

I had to say something now. But his eyes were so pale, I stumbled over my words. "I have been fortunate to have Lady, I mean, Aunt Frances for my teacher. She has taught me everything I know."

Marchand smiled. "You must have good skills after seven years at her side."

Before I had time to ask myself how he knew when I had come to Hawkstone, he put a goblet of red wine into my hand.

"Tell me," said Marchand smoothly. "Would you advise comfrey with liquorice above horehound and honey for a spring chill?"

I sipped the wine and the words stuck in my throat. This was my uncle's finest Burgundy and I knew he had been keeping it to celebrate Arabella's marriage when it took place.

Pierre Marchand watched my face. "A fine wine indeed, my dear. Sir Charles must approve of your betrothal."

"You are wrong, sir," I said sharply. "This wine is intended for Arabella. The steward has drawn from the wrong barrel."

Everything was upside-down. If my uncle had indeed chosen the Burgundy specially, why had he called Suckley an oaf when he thought no one would hear him?

The Frenchman lifted his glass to me in a mock toast; he seemed to know that I was thinking about Suckley. Then he turned as if he had eyes in the back of his head.

Aunt Frances was glaring at me. I should have been talking to Suckley instead of leaving him to Arabella but I couldn't bring myself to stay near him. Now it was time to go through to the Great Chamber for supper and she wanted me to go in with him. I held her gaze but didn't move.

Marchand bowed to me. "I would be honoured to accompany you, madam," he said.

The white walls of the Great Chamber gleamed in the light thrown out from the fire. It was a huge room full of a sense of importance and decorated with family emblems painted in bright colours. When I had first come to Hawkstone, I had been terrified of walking into this room so my aunt had pointed out to me all the tiny plasterwork animals that were carved on the walls. She told me to choose two who would be my secret friends.

Now, as I walked the length of the Chamber, I ignored its grandness and looked for the tiny, fat bear carved above the window and the owl sitting in a pear tree on the wall opposite the fire.

At that moment, it seemed to me that they were the only friends I had.

We took our places at a heavy oak table laid with more candles than there had been at Christmas. My aunt's best silver plate was on show and there were Venetian crystal goblets at each place. Carved ivory animals with precious stones for eyes were arranged in a pattern down the middle.

Whatever my aunt and uncle might think of Suckley privately, they appeared to be trying very hard to impress him.

As Lord Suckley took his place beside me, he grunted as his eyes strayed to my bodice. It would have been laughable if it hadn't been so disgusting. It was as if he was an animal sniffing a scent that aroused him.

Sarah stood by the sideboard with a ewer full of hot water in one hand and a bowl in the other. A clean linen napkin hung over her arm. I hoped with all of my heart that she had remembered our conversation that morning.

I watched as Lord Suckley dipped his hands into the bowl and wiped his fingers on the linen cloth. After he'd finished, it was too dirty to offer to anyone else. I saw Sarah frown and take a clean cloth from her apron.

There was a clatter of wooden soles as two servants came into the room, each carrying one end of a long trencher. The pike I had caught lay in a pool of green sauce, sprinkled with capers and parsley and ground pepper. The skin along the body had been removed and the flesh coated with some kind of shiny brown syrup. The head and tail were decorated with violets and cowslips. It looked nothing like the pike that had been swimming in the river, and I felt a pang of guilt for ending its life.

Lord Suckley leaned forward, smacking his lips. "Of all dishes, this one is my favourite," he announced, more to himself than anyone else. He cut himself a big fillet of pike and scooped it on to his trencher. Then he spooned so much caper sauce over the top that it dripped on to the table.

Opposite, Arabella was watching us with obvious delight. She picked up the salter, which was a silver miniature of the ship Richard sailed on, and pushed it towards Suckley. "*The Pigeon* sails towards you with Richard at the helm, my lord," she cried, choking with laughter.

Aunt Frances frowned. "I see no reason for your merriment, daughter," she said sharply. "We are all disappointed that Richard can't be with us on this important occasion."

She turned to me. "Do you have any news of him, Emerald?"

"I haven't heard from Richard in months, Aunt," I replied coldly. "You know that."

"Who is Richard?" asked Suckley through a mouthful of boiled pike.

49

The table went silent.

"I beg your pardon, my lord?" asked my uncle with a look of astonishment on his face.

"Richard who?" said Suckley, in a louder voice, as he took a fingerful of salt from the salter and spread it thickly over the fish.

"My Lord Suckley," said Uncle Charles. "Am I to understand that you know nothing of Sir Richard St John, son of the late Lord Stephen St John?"

"His lordship forgets, Sir Charles," said Pierre Marchand quickly.

"I forget nothing, Marchand," snarled Suckley. He dunked his bread into the sauce and splashed more on to the table.

We watched in disgust as Suckley mopped the drips straight from the table and pushed the bread into his mouth.

"Young St John is of no importance to me," said Suckley, spraying wet crumbs in front of him. "It makes no odds if he is afloat or on land."

Uncle Charles stared at him. "Surely it would be courteous to know something of Emerald's brother?" he said.

Suckley shrugged. "A man of my age can't waste his time with courtesy." He leered at me. "There's a job needs doing and 'twere best done quickly."

Once again, I saw the bull in the field of cows and I was so repulsed bile rushed up my throat.

"Baked hen, my lord," said Sarah. As she set down a

whole bird in front of him, she caught my eye and gave me the faintest of winks.

Knowing that Suckley was about to eat a plate of rotten meat laced with gut gripe made me instantly feel better and I made up my mind to encourage him to swallow as much as he could. I leaned towards him and licked the tips of my fingers one by one. "Cook's hen is even tastier than her pike," I whispered.

Suckley's eyes were out on stalks. "I shall have it to please you," he said, grunting and wiping the sweat from his face. I speared the bird with my own knife, eased it on to Suckley's trencher and smiled into his piggy eyes. "You do me a great honour, sir," I said with a husky whisper, but in truth I wanted to shout out loud with laughter.

Chapter Four

"Up all night in the jakes was the lordy lord." Meg pulled apart the bed curtains and set down bread and a mug of hot, spicy milk on my table. "Sarah says I'm to tell you that special."

I let a grin spread over my face as I remembered the sight of Suckley stuffing himself to impress me. In the end, he had eaten the whole hen.

I sat up and drank the milk as Meg pulled back the shutters, then shook out my cotton petticoat and woollen gown. It was barely dawn, and my plan was to get down to the stables and see Molly before the rest of the household was about. No doubt Marchand would have wormwood with him to ease Suckley's gripe, so I couldn't count on him being unwell for the rest of the morning.

"Saw Tom in the kitchen," said Meg, as she untied my cap and began to spread my hair over my shoulders. "He says that French dog has been down in the stables asking questions."

"What kind of questions?"

"Wants to know what Molly eats. And why her coat's so shiny." Meg looked away.

"What else?" I asked. "I know you're hiding something." I pushed the bread towards her. "Eat it. I'm not hungry."

Meg took the bread and squeezed it in her hand. "'E wanted to know when she was going to the pits."

At first I couldn't think what she was talking about. What pits? Stone pits? Mud pits? Then I understood, and my stomach turned over.

"Did he mean *bear* pits?"

Meg nodded uncomfortably.

"What did Tom say?" I demanded.

"That Molly wasn't a sport animal and he should mind his own business."

Meg brought the bread to her mouth but couldn't swallow it. "The French dog said it *was* his business since he's a loyal servant to the Queen and everyone knows her opinion of bears and they ain't pets."

"What business is it of Marchand's what the Queen thinks?"

Meg shrugged. "He's a troublemakcr, miss," she said. "That's what Tom said."

Arabella had told me about the Queen's bear pits. She kept her own mastiffs and loved to watch them tearing apart half-starved animals whose claws had been ripped out and whose teeth had been broken. It was cruel and disgusting and I couldn't understand how the Queen could enjoy it. Even her courtiers stayed away if they had a chance.

"You daft bumpkin," Arabella had sneered at me. "Don't you understand? The Queen's cruel. The *world*'s cruel. That's the way of it."

My hands were shaking as I pulled my woollen clothes on over my shift. There was no time to step into bodices and tie up laces. "Where is Marchand now?"

"In the herb store."

"Why?" I asked sharply.

"He's making a remedy for the lordy lord's guts," said Meg.

I strapped up my boots and pushed two combs into my hair. It was odd that a herbalist should travel without any common remedies. I thought of his colourless eyes and shivered again. "If anyone asks, tell them my bed was empty when you came in." I ran towards the door and crashed headlong into Arabella, who was dressed in the lambskin cape and purple woollen shawl she always wore on her journeys to London.

"God's death, Arabella!" I cried. "What—?" but the words stopped in my mouth when I saw her face. It was bright red, and contorted as if she was in some kind of agony. She shoved a piece of parchment at my stomach and lurched across the room, moaning like a wounded animal.

"The devil has her, miss," cried Meg. "I've seen it before!"

"Shut up," I said. "You'll wake the whole house, if Arabella hasn't already!" I shoved the parchment down the front of my dress and hauled Arabella over to the bed.

"Get some brandy from the cupboard!"

I locked Arabella's head against my chest to keep her still while Meg tipped the liquor into her mouth.

Arabella choked and the brandy dribbled down her chin and the front of her cape, but she stopped shaking.

I loosened my grasp and gave her more brandy. I had to calm her down before Hetty spread the story through the house.

Meg held out the bottle again, but I shook my head. "Go now – and not a word of what you've seen."

Meg coloured. "You can trust me, miss," she said, setting the bottle on the table and shutting the door behind her.

I took the scroll from my dress.

"What does this say?" I asked Arabella, who lay on my bed, staring at the wall.

"I am banished from the Court," replied Arabella in a flat voice.

At first I didn't take in what this would mean to Arabella. From what she'd told me, people were banished from Court all the time. Then slowly I began to understand this was a catastrophe. Arabella's whole life was centred around the Court in London. It was what she lived for and, in truth, it was all she had. To be exiled in the country would be worse than death for her.

"Why?" I asked.

Arabella blew through her lips. "Because I am stupid. I let my soft heart get the better of me. I helped Anne Swithin hide her marriage from the Queen." She took a swig of brandy. The colour was coming back to her face. "Onion-eyed whore," muttered Arabella. "She didn't tell me she was pregnant."

Arabella took the scroll and unrolled it. "See for yourself. There is the Queen's hand."

I stared at the spidery *Elizabeth R* and the inky print of her stamp, and shivered. "How long will she banish you?"

"Until I can find someone to speak on my behalf." Arabella yanked at the ties on her cape. "And how can I do that buried here in a dung heap in Wales?"

"Who else knows?"

"The Queen wrote to my father. I suspect that worm of a Frenchman knows, too. He's been asking enough questions. And not just about me." She looked down at her red leather gloves and began to pull them off, finger by finger. "By the way, I meant to congratulate you on last night."

"*What?*" Her mood had changed so quickly it caught me by surprise.

"Poisoning the old goat's supper," said Arabella. "It was a touch of genius."

Hairs rose on the back of my neck. A voice in my mind said, *Don't trust her.*

"There was no poisoning done. The hen must have been rotten."

Arabella raised her eyebrows. "Strange it was the one Sarah put in front of him."

I felt the blood drain from my face.

"Don't worry," said Arabella. "It was only me that saw her wink, unless that Frenchman has eyes in the back of his head. Thanks for the brandy." She shook her head. "It was the shock of it. I'll be better now."

But it was clear Arabella was only pretending. Her face had gone grey and her lips began to tremble again. Suddenly she grabbed my hand. "God help me, Emerald. What am I going to do?"

"Summer is coming," I said. I wanted to be encouraging, but I heard my voice sounding hollow. "We could ride out if you want."

It was odd. I surprised myself by feeling sorry for Arabella. Then I remembered what Sarah had said and maybe she was right. If Arabella took it into her head to use her cunning to thwart Suckley, I could play for time until Richard came back. But why would she suddenly want to help me? It would break the habit of a lifetime.

In the end it was Arabella who made up my mind for me. "I have an idea that might suit us both," she said. She cocked her head like a bird – though she looked more like a hungry gull than a kindly robin.

"It seems to me," said Arabella briskly, "that if I am to

57

be marooned here for a few weeks, I might as well keep busy. So why don't I teach you a few dance steps and some card games? I know all the Court favourites." She patted my hand and said carefully, "If you do become a Lady, you'll need to know how to behave like one. And even if you don't marry him, Suckley will think you're cooperating with him and then at least you can play for time until Richard comes back."

I nodded warily. "Do you think you'll be here for that long?"

"God knows." Arabella shrugged and pulled a face. "It depends how many men of influence pass by."

I knew she was trying to be funny, but it didn't work. She only sounded more desperate.

"Would Uncle Charles plead your case?"

Arabella shook her head. "He didn't want me to leave Hawkstone in the first place." She poured some brandy into a pewter mug and set it in front of me. Then she lifted the bottle. "Shall we be sisters, then?"

I took the mug. "Sisters," I said and swallowed the burning liquid in one gulp.

Tears poured down my cheeks and, as I choked and spluttered, I heard Arabella roaring with laughter.

"Lucky for you, ladies don't drink much at Court," she cried. "Else you'd be under the table before supper was served!"

I laughed and wiped my dripping nose on my sleeve.

For the first time ever, I felt the queerest attachment to Arabella.

It was Arabella's idea that I introduce Molly to Suckley. She began to think up a plan almost as soon as I set down my mug.

"It's the only way to keep her safe if he becomes your husband," said Arabella.

"That's madness," I replied. I told her what Marchand had said about the Queen's opinion of bears. And Suckley was supposed to pride himself on being a loyal servant to the Crown.

"Who cares what the Queen says?" said Arabella. "She is not interested in some country wife's pet bear." She paused. "Begging your pardon, my dear. And as for Marchand, he's nothing but a nosy Frenchman. It's Suckley you have to win over and the only way is to flatter him. Then you can play for time."

I didn't like the idea. Even if I did make Suckley understand that Molly was gentle and nothing more than a pet, I couldn't see how it would change things. From his lecherous looks and grunting noises, it was clear he only wanted to get me on my own as soon as possible.

"Trust me," said Arabella. "You have to *appear* willing, otherwise you'll be his wife before you even have a chance to get out of it."

In the end that's what persuaded me to go along with

her. And if it didn't work out, I told myself there was nothing to lose. Arabella was right. I had to show willing.

"All right," I said. "I'll do it."

Arabella patted my knee and her eyes were bright and excited. "Good," she cried. "And remember to wear red."

I stared at her. "Why should I wear red?"

"Because red cures sickness," said Arabella, rolling her eyes as if she was talking to a child. "You can say you chose it to soothe his gripe."

"That's ridiculous."

"Nothing's ridiculous if you want something," said Arabella sharply. She held my eyes with an even gaze. "The old goat will be eating out of your hand. Take my word for it."

And, like a fool, I did.

An hour later, I was sitting on a turf seat in Aunt Frances' garden dressed in a red woollen skirt and jacket, with Molly's head resting in my lap. "Be a good bear," I said, digging my fingers into her fur. "Suckley's worse than a rat. But you mustn't eat him."

Molly grunted and I bent down to breathe in her sharp, musky smell.

It wasn't until I saw the shadow on the gravel path that I realised Suckley was standing behind me. "My lord!" I jumped up from the bench, yanking Molly's rope in my surprise. "I beg your pardon! I had no idea you were there." From the look on his face, I was sure he'd heard what I'd said.

"How unbecoming that a young woman should prefer the company of a bear to the company of her suitor." His voice was thin and unpleasant.

"Molly is more than a bear, sir." I spoke as sweetly as I could manage. "She's a pet to me." I pressed my foot against Molly's haunches. She sat down without once taking her eyes away from Suckley's face.

"A bear on a rope belongs in a pit," said Suckley, turning away from Molly's gaze. "Marchand is right. She would make a fine gift to the Queen's mastiffs."

I forgot everything Arabella told me.

"You're *loathsome*!" I shouted.

"Hussy!" snapped Suckley. He sniffed wetly and spat on the ground. "But you shall be my wife before the summer's out, and then I'll tame you, just you wait."

"I would rather be a nun," I said, in a voice that shook with rage.

"Sugar cakes, my lord?" Arabella appeared out of nowhere. "I baked them with liquorice to soothe your stomach." As she spoke, I felt her foot touch mine as if to tell me she would look after things now.

I saw her smile into Suckley's angry face. "Emerald has looked after Molly since she was a cub, my lord," she said soothingly. "You must understand she feels a great affection for her."

"I understand she's a hoyden," snorted Suckley. He

flicked his fingers at me. "I'll not allow it." As his hand moved, Molly bared her teeth and growled. It wasn't a threatening noise, and Arabella had heard Molly growl many times before. To my astonishment, she suddenly screamed as if she was being attacked. The next moment the cakes fell from her basket and Molly lumbered past her to eat them up.

Arabella screamed again and tried to push Molly away, as if the bear was trying to attack her.

I was completely taken aback. "Arabella!" I shouted. "Leave her be!"

But Arabella appeared not to hear me and and threw herself against Suckley's chest, while Molly began to eat up the sugar cakes. "Save me, my lord!," cried Arabella. "Save me!"

My jaw dropped. *What on earth was going on?*

"Get out of my way, idiot woman!" Suckley pushed Arabella away and smashed his boot into Molly's snout.

Blood spurted from Molly's mouth, and she yelped with pain and surprise.

"Leave her alone!" I yelled. "It's the cakes she wants."

I tightened my grip on Molly's rope and yanked her sideways as Suckley aimed his next kick at her head.

"God damn that bear!" he roared, pulling a small sword from his belt. "I'll have her ears before I kill her!"

Molly stood up on her hind legs and bellowed. She was terrified and angry, but I knew that if she touched a single hair on Suckley's head, he would insist she be killed.

I picked up a cake, rubbed it on her nose, and threw it as hard as I could towards the gate. For a second, she hesitated. Then I yanked the rope and she followed me as I ran back down the path towards the stables.

"Hurry, Molly, hurry!" My breath caught in my throat. For a terrible moment, I thought my legs would give way beneath me.

"That bear is mine!" roared Suckley. Behind me, I heard the crunch of his boots on the gravel as he began to chase after us.

"No, my lord! Stop! I beg you!" cried Arabella. "You'll be hurt." Even as I ran, I noticed that there was no fright in her voice. It was almost as if she was pretending to be a damsel in distress.

Then suddenly I understood and fury surged through me. It was Arabella who intended to flatter Suckley so he'd help her get back to Court. And she'd set up Molly and me to give her the chance to do it. How could I have been stupid enough to trust her?

I slipped on a lump of dung and fell forwards, crashing face first on to the cobbled yard.

My head hurt so much I wanted to be sick. Then all I can remember was a thick stink of ferret and blackness.

When I opened my eyes, I was worried about two things: first, Molly, then my teeth. I've always been rather proud of my teeth. They are white and even and I make a point of cleaning them every day with a rag and sweet vinegar. I ran my tongue nervously inside my mouth, to make sure they were all still there.

"Counting yer teeth, are ya?" Meg's beady face appeared in front of me. "You ain't broke nothing. Just whacked yer 'ead. You bin out cold for an hour. We was worried."

"Where's Molly?"

"Safe and sound in her stable. Wanna feel your bump?" Meg guided my fingers to a lump above my right ear. "It's a good 'un."

I was recognising things now. I was in my bed, back in my room.

A strong smell of ferret hung in the air. "Has Tom been here?"

Meg laughed. Tom was famous for his stink. He called his ferrets after kings of England, and carried them around in an inside pocket of his smock. "Carried you all the way back like a babe in arms," said Meg.

She smeared a cloth in grease and rubbed it gently on to my bruise. "Cook started to scream you was dead, but Sarah told Tom to bring you up here."

I gulped down a mugful of elderflower cordial. "Suckley kicked Molly."

"I know." Meg patted my hand. "Lucky I was taking some carrots to the stables. I gave the stable boy some for Molly and she settled quick enough."

Meg suddenly jumped up, opened the door and looked both ways down the corridor. Then she came back to my side. "But never mind the carrots, miss!" she said in an excited whisper. "I seen 'em through the hedge."

The hairs on the back of my neck began to prickle.

"Who did you see?" I asked.

"The maggoty ape and her fanciness," replied Meg.

"Do you mean you saw Arabella and Lord Suckley?" I could barely put the words together in my mouth.

Meg wagged her head up and down. "Squashed up like squabs together! Kissin', they was!"

"*Kissing*?" I yelped. I stared at her. "What are you talking about?"

Meg frowned. "You know," she said. She made kissing noises on the back of her hand. "Like that."

Footsteps sounded in the corridor.

My head was whirling. I fell back against my pillows and put my hands over my face. "Whoever it is, tell them I'm sick."

"Don't you worry, miss," said Meg. "I'll get rid of 'em."

There was a single knock and my uncle walked into the room.

"Miss Emerald's right poorly, sir," cried Meg, holding her arms out to bar his way. "Beggin' yer pardon, my lord. Ladyship said no one's to worry her."

Through my fingers, I saw Uncles Charles wave his arm impatiently. "I'll be the judge of that, Meg Catchpole," he snapped. "Back to the kitchen with you."

I didn't take my hands from my face as Uncle Charles sat down on a chair beside me. "I have something to say to you, Emerald," he said. His voice was calmer than I had expected. I dropped my hands and sat up.

"If it's about Molly, she only growled because of the cakes. Then Suckley kicked her and would have cut off her ears if I hadn't pulled her away." I was surprised to see that he was still listening. "She would have had his leg if I'd stayed."

"The man's an idiot," said my uncle shortly. "I came to say I don't blame you for what happened with Molly." He paused. "Although Arabella's taken to her bed with the shock of it all."

I thought my head would explode with fury. What was he talking about? Arabella was a hypocrite and a liar and a bawd! She was as bad as Suckley! It took every bit of strength left in me to hide my feelings from him. "I'll make my apologies to his lordship," I muttered.

"It's too late for that," said my uncle. "Suckley's gone."

I sat up with a jerk. "Gone *where?*"

My uncle shrugged. "He didn't have the courtesy to say goodbye. Nor his perfumier either."

I stared stupidly at him.

"Surely Lord Suckley spoke to Arabella before he left?"

Uncle Charles looked at me strangely. "Why would he do that? He has nothing to do with Arabella."

What Meg had seen through the hedge filled my mind. I turned away so my uncle wouldn't see my face.

"Arabella was the last to see him," I said in a stony voice. "He must have told her why he was leaving."

66

"God's death, Emerald," cried my uncle suddenly. "Stop talking like a fool. Suckley is a graceless boor, but if you're thinking you can get out of marrying him you're wrong. Nothing can change it, and the sooner you accept that, the better it will be for all of us." He strode out of the room and slammed the door behind him.

Chapter Five

The next morning Arabella left to visit cousins in Cardiff. No one except me could understand why she wanted to stay with a family who had small children and kept hunting hounds in their bedchamber, but I said nothing. I would have slapped her black and blue if I had seen her, and she knew it.

That afternoon a message came from Richard that *The Pigeon* had dropped anchor off Calais. I wrote to him immediately. Then I spent the rest of the month imagining the letter travelling on the mail coach all the way to Dover and across the Channel to Calais by ship.

I was sure Richard would come to me as soon as my letter reached him. But May passed and turned into June and nothing happened and, almost every day, I thought of how Arabella had betrayed me. I would never forget her pretty smiles and false screams and the way she had clutched at Suckley's doublet and begged him to save her from Molly's jaws.

Then one afternoon I came into the Great Chamber and Arabella and her mother were sitting by the window embroidering hassocks. There was a strange, strained feeling in the room and I felt sure they had been arguing. As I entered, Aunt Frances stood up.

"I will not have my house turned into a battlefield," she said, looking at us both. "Whatever is going on between you two, you will settle it right now."

At that moment, Hetty opened the door. "Beggin' your pardon, mistress." She bobbed in front of my aunt. "There's a messenger outside from London."

Arabella's head jerked up.

"Does he have letters for me?" she demanded.

"No, my lady."

Arabella threw down her hassock. "Then get out of my sight, slut!" she shouted furiously.

"Arabella!" snapped Aunt Frances. "What *is* wrong with you?"

"Nothing," replied Arabella. She picked up her hassock. "I *hate* embroidery."

Aunt Frances stared at her and then at me. "I'm sick to my stomach with both of you," she shouted. Then she left the Chamber, slamming the door behind her.

I sat down by the window, determined not to be the first one to speak.

"That foul toad," muttered Arabella. "I hate him!" She stabbed at her embroidery and pricked her thumb with the needle. "Ow!"

I looked up. "Who do you hate?" They were the first words we had exchanged for almost six weeks.

"Suckley, of course," said Arabella, sucking her thumb. "I'm sorry for you, Emerald, truly I am."

"Stop talking in riddles, Arabella," I replied furiously. "Tell me the truth or I swear to God, I'll slap you."

Arabella went white and she hunched back in her chair.

"The oaf promised to help me get back to Court," she said. "He said he'd speak to Lord Henry of Orgon. Your precious mother's husband."

I was stunned – this was the last thing I'd expected to hear.

"What's Lord Henry got to do with your banishment?"

"He has the Queen's ear," said Arabella. "And now that Suckley is on such good terms with your mother, he said he would write to Lord Henry and ask him to put in a good word for me with the Queen." She paused. "You might as well know that the Queen has accepted an invitation to visit Bleathwood this summer."

I stared at her. "Why should that concern me?"

Arabella looked sideways at me. "Because your mother has arranged for you and Suckley to be married at the same time."

"What?" I stared at her with my mouth hanging open. "Why didn't anyone tell me?"

Her words clattered around my head like stones in a bucket. "Are you making this up?"

"Certainly not," snapped Arabella. 'I'm doing you a favour since no one appears to have told you."

I looked at her in disgust. "When did you find this out?"

"Suckley told me," replied Arabella. "Apparently the Queen's visit was your mother's doing. And Suckley planned to announce your marriage on his last evening here." She shrugged. "But after you and your bear managed to humiliate him, he decided to leave."

I stood up and walked over to the window. Through the leaded glass, the lilac bushes were in blossom and, beyond, the fields glinted green with wheat. "You set the whole thing up," I said in a hollow voice. "You wanted to flatter him. You didn't care about me." I heard Meg's words in my head. *Squashed up like squabs together.*

"He promised to help me," muttered Arabella.

My anger boiled over. "I'm not surprised after the show you put on for him," I yelled. "What else did you do?"

"I allowed him to seduce me," replied Arabella flatly. She looked at me with cold eyes. "I let him bruise me and make me bleed. Is that what you want to hear?"

I felt as if I was falling over a cliff.

"Don't look at me like that, you prissy little fool," shouted Arabella. "He is the only person I know who can get me back to Court! What else was I supposed to do?"

I sat down on a stool and buried my head in my hands.

"There's going to be a baby." I heard Arabella's voice like it was a fly buzzing at the window. "I want you to help me get rid of it."

The voice turned into a sob. "Help me, Emerald. You're the only person I can turn to."

71

I looked up at her. "How could you let him touch you?" I whispered.

Arabella shook her head. "Help me," she said again.

"What about your baby?"

"It's Suckley's spawn," muttered Arabella. "I don't call that human."

The air was thick between us. Two months ago, I would have left Arabella on her own. But now everything was more nasty than I could have ever imagined, and I knew it would only get nastier while my mother's influence was on the rise. If I was going to survive her, I had to grow up.

Maybe Arabella was right. Maybe I *was* a prissy little fool.

When I opened my mouth, it was as if my voice was coming from the bottom of a well. "There's a woman called Ma Wipeweed," I said.

Aunt Frances had told me about Ma Wipeweed. While her visitors waited outside, Ma Wipeweed boiled a cauldron of soured milk mixed with rue, hyssop and three handfuls of a black, jelly-like soap she kept in a tub. Two steaming hot jugs of this foul liquid had to be swallowed at once, followed by a bowl of chopped green hay and a glass of unfermented beer. The vomiting was so terrible, it was supposed to make the womb go into shock and expel what was inside it.

I made myself look straight into Arabella's face. "She makes a potion," I said. "The last two unfortunates that went to her were buried in a plague pit. No church would have them."

Arabella folded up her embroidery. "What odds? I'm as good as dead if I have this baby, anyway. I don't care where they dump me." She buried her face in her hands.

Then there was a clatter of horses' hooves on the cobbles, and the voice I had been dreaming about for so long floated through the window. "Meg! You little urchin! Here's a penny. Run and tell my sister I'm back from the sea!"

Arabella grabbed my arm and held it tightly. "Say nothing to anyone," she said harshly. "Promise me."

A pain went through my middle at the thought of the helpless baby inside Arabella's body. It was the devil's work to even think of harming it, but I knew she would have found out about Ma Wipeweed one way or another. I only wished it hadn't been me that told her.

I could smell sick on Arabella's breath and wondered if Aunt Frances had noticed. "I'll say nothing," I told her, pulling my arm away. "Now leave me to welcome my brother."

It wasn't how I had hoped to see Richard again. After being with Arabella, I felt like I needed to sit in a hot bath and scrub myself clean.

I ran to the great oak door and waited, half-hidden inside the stone porch.

Two men dressed in tight-waisted woollen doublets sat astride their horses, their long cloaks spread in bedraggled circles behind them.

I watched from my hiding place as they swung down from their saddles and landed lightly on the ground. Anyone could see they had come a long way. The horses' legs were caked with mud and their haunches were lathered with sweat. I let my eyes move from the horses to my brother's face. After all the time I had waited, I wanted to take things slowly. I had never seen Richard dressed in anything other than brown or black. Now he looked quite the man of fashion in a high, black hat with a red feather and matching red hose.

I listened as he laughed and joked with his companion and I wished I wasn't wearing my aunt's hand-me-down kirtle with my hair pulled back under a worn, white linen cap. It made me feel like a coarse country girl and I didn't want him to be ashamed of me.

"Sister!" Richard turned and saw me standing in the porch. He threw open his arms and strode towards me. "Surely you're not shy?"

"Of course not," I said, smiling. "I was merely admiring your clothes. Something of a courtier, I see."

Richard flung his arms round me. Even through the sweat of his journey, I could smell the sea on him. And I was so happy to see him that I clung to him like a limpet. We stood together for a long time. At last I let him go. I stood back and stared into his ruddy, bearded face. Richard was shorter than me, and stocky, like our father. Really, the only feature we had in common was the colour of our hair. Even then, mine was wavy and thick and his was straight. "Did my letter reach you?"

"Yes." He hugged me again and whispered in my ear. "We shall talk later."

I took Richard's arm and leaned against him as we walked back towards the horses. I wanted to tell him how long I had been waiting and hoping, but in the end I couldn't speak. I just held on to him.

"Sam here says Suckley's a cross between a pig and a weasel," said Richard, patting my arm. "I'm not having my only sister married to that. Sam, may I present my sister, Emerald. Emerald, this is my friend Sam Pemberton." He grinned. "Actually, Sam's a viscount, but we don't bother with ceremony!"

I let go of Richard and made a short curtsey in front of a blond man with full lips and the most beautiful violet eyes. When he smiled, his teeth were straight and white, and his eyes smiled, too.

"I am honoured," said Sam Pemberton, taking my hand and holding it lightly. "Richard tells me you speak French and Spanish. Where did you learn?"

"I learnt it here," I replied. His face made me want to smile back at him. "My governess was French, but spoke many other languages." I shrugged and held his eyes. "Except English. I taught her that."

Richard laughed. "I swear to you, Sam, Emerald is the cleverest woman I have ever met. She only has to hear something once and she remembers it."

"A useful talent," said Sam Pemberton quietly. "Can you remember what you read as well?"

"Of course she can!" said Richard before I had a chance to speak. "Which is why she mustn't be wasted on a pig."

To my surprise, Sam blushed. There was something frank and open about him. I found I was taking to him already. "Enough, Richard," he said, glancing at me. "I'm sure none of us wish to speak of my Lord Suckley. It is too fine a day."

I held out my hand to Richard and stood on the first step up to the open front door. "Come inside. You will be thirsty after your journey."

"Ale, gentlemen?" Arabella stood at the top of the steps holding out two large pewter tankards. She looked completely different from the person I had left sitting with her face in her hands in the Great Chamber. Her hair was dressed with flowers, and she wore a low-cut dress in a green leaf pattern, showing the bluish-white mounds of her breasts. The pallor of her face was hidden under the rouge on her cheeks.

"Why, Richard! What fine clothes! I wouldn't know you for a sea dog!" Arabella set down the tankards and kissed Richard on the cheek. "I am so pleased to see you. I swear Emerald and I have talked about nothing else these last two months."

"Two months, Arabella?" Richard raised his eyebrows. "How can our Queen spare you?"

Arabella gave a false smile and patted his arm prettily. "It's a long story, and when I've the time I'll tell it you." She turned and curtsied at Sam Pemberton. "Excuse me, my lord."

"Faith, I've the manners of a bullock!" cried Richard. "Sam, this is Arabella Mount. My guardian's daughter. We are old friends from childhood."

I watched Sam bow and take the hand that Arabella had offered him. "It is an honour, madam," he said. "Lord Chesham tells me you play the best hand of gleek at Court."

Arabella's eyes flashed in surprise. "My Lord Chesham flatters me," she replied. "'Tis the Queen who is the best player – although woe betide the subject who does not have a purse to hand to pay their debt!"

Sam laughed. "I have heard the same story, my lady. Except when the debt is hers."

Arabella's eyes widened. "Do you play the Queen, sir?"

"Certainly not," replied Sam. "That is far too dangerous an occupation for a poor sailor."

"But you are acquainted with Lord Chesham," said Arabella.

"Indeed," replied Sam. "I was his clerk for a time and helped with the translation of French law for the Crown."

Arabella's face shone. "Then you know Lady Farquhar and Lord Henderson!" she cried. "They are close friends of mine."

Arabella put her arm through his and when she looked at me, there was a wolfish grin on her face.

I hung back to speak with Richard on my own. I wanted to talk to him before anyone else did, but at that moment Uncle Charles appeared through the stone arch, coming in from the garden.

He hadn't seen us and I pulled Richard towards me. "Brother, please, I must talk to you before you speak to our guardians."

But Richard shook me off gently and was already crossing the cobblestone yard, shouting out a greeting.

Chapter Six

That evening, at Arabella's special request, musicians were summoned to the Hall and there was dancing after supper. While my aunt sat by the fire with her embroidery and my uncle sat with his steward, Arabella made a great show of taking me through the graceful steps of a pavane in front of Richard and Sam.

"The Queen knows all the steps, my dear," whispered Arabella, as she held my hand high and led me across the floor. "And she values a good dancer. Mark my words, if you ever need to get her attention, dance well and she will notice you."

At the time, I thought nothing of this. As it turned out, it was some of the best advice Arabella ever gave me and, later, it would change the course of my life.

Towards the end of the evening in the Hall, when flagons of wine had come and gone and the table was littered with orange peel and sweetmeats, Uncle Charles finally agreed to dance. He chose a slow saraband. We watched as he and my aunt stepped gracefully up and down the floor, their fingertips touching as they turned towards each other in wide, sweeping circles.

I hadn't seen the two of them dance for many years. As I looked at them, it occurred to me that the formality of the music and the separateness of the dance steps suited the way they led their lives together.

A hand tapped my shoulder. "I have a bet with your brother that you trip over in the next dance." Sam Pemberton stood in front of me. "It's a saltarello." He bent and I felt his breath in my ear as he whispered, "Richard's given them a sovereign to play it."

"Is it fast or slow?"

"Fast. Follow my lead."

I caught Richard's eye, and he raised his glass of wine. He was laughing, and his face shone like it always did when he was about to play a trick on me. Beside him, Arabella held her hand to her lips to hide her own laughter. She had been trying to flirt with Sam for much of the evening, but now she had switched her attention to Richard, and it was clear that he was enjoying it.

Sam guided me on to the floor. "Start on the inside foot then step, step, step, hop. You will soon master it."

"I won't remember," I whispered.

"Yes, you will," said Sam. "Listen to the tune and your feet will do the rest."

The musicians stood up and played a tune that leaped and jiggled in the air like water bubbling over rocks. When the flute joined in over the top, Sam took my hand and we began to dance and something happened that I hadn't expected.

Of course I had danced with men before, at Christmas and May Day celebrations, but it was always the steps of the dance that had been uppermost in my mind and I worried that I would appear clumsy or dance out of time to the music. But as soon as Sam took me in his arms, it was as if our bodies had always known each other and it was the most natural thing in the world to lean towards him and let him guide me.

"You smell of roses," whispered Sam in my ear as we spun round and surged down the room.

"And you smell of horses," I replied. I almost laughed out loud. How could I have said that to a complete stranger? But somehow we felt anything but strangers – and from the spark in Sam's eyes as he looked at me, I knew he felt the same.

I heard Sam chortle as he pulled me tight to his chest and we flung ourselves up and down the room as the musicians played faster and faster. As I ducked underneath Sam's arm, I suddenly saw Arabella watching us. She wasn't smiling any more and her lips were pressed together into a hard, thin line. Then, with a jerk of her head, she turned back towards Richard and I saw a wide, encouraging smile spread across her face.

I stumbled, but Sam caught me.

"What's wrong?" he whispered. Then he followed my eyes and saw Arabella's face.

"She's jealous of you, my dear," he said simply. "Pay her no heed. She can't hurt you."

But he was wrong. I could read Arabella like a book. She had seen the look on Sam's face as we had danced and in that moment, gambler that she was, she had changed her mind. With Suckley's child in her belly and time running out, she needed someone to fall back on if everything else failed. Richard for a husband was the best she was going to get.

I stumbled again.

Sam lifted me up and swung me in a circle, so I could pick up the steps before my feet touched the floor again. Then, as if he had been reading my thoughts, he leaned towards me as the music played around us and said, "Richard's not a fool."

But men don't know women as well as other women do. Sam had seen enough of Arabella to recognise her kind, but even he could never have guessed what was driving her plan forward.

After that evening, everything changed very quickly. For the next two days, I watched Richard follow Arabella around with an idiotic, lopsided grin on his face, and every time I tried to speak to him on his own, he made some excuse and I remembered how he'd left me to greet Uncle Charles. It made me think of what my aunt had said about my mother being a dangerous enemy to Richard. Although I had no idea what she was talking about, for the first time, I wondered if Richard was actually trying to avoid me. I had always assumed he would have a plan to stop my marriage to Suckley and from what he'd said, he disliked him as much as I did. But days had passed and he'd said nothing more.

It made me sick at heart to think it, but perhaps Richard really *was* afraid of our mother's influence over him. But surely he wouldn't sacrifice his own sister for the sake of an easy life?

On the third day I rose early and waited for Richard to come down the stairs into the Hall. I knew Arabella never left her bedroom until mid-morning, and as soon as I saw him, I ran over and grabbed his arm and led him into a corner of the garden.

At first Richard thought I was up to some kind of prank and laughingly pulled his arm back. Then he saw the look on my face and kept up with me.

When we came to the end of the first yew hedge, a good few hundred paces from the house, he stopped. "What's wrong?" he said.

"*Wrong*?" I replied in a low, fierce voice. "Richard! Have you lost your wits? Every time I try to talk to you, you run away."

My anger was so full of sadness and hurt, I found myself crying. "I thought you came home to help me!" I said in a choked voice. "All you've done is chase after Arabella! Don't you care about what is to happen to me?"

Richard stared stupidly. "I'm sorry. I've not meant to be

unkind. It's…" He gave me that same lopsided grin. "Well
… it's Arabella. I've never thought of her much before and
now I think of her all the time. I can't help it. I'm sorry. I've
neglected you. We need to talk about this, uh, proposal."

I wiped my eyes and breathed deeply to steady my
voice. "You have to stop this marriage," I said. "I would
rather go to a convent than let that scabby ape touch me."

Richard pulled a face and looked away. I could see I had
embarrassed him. I was so upset I nearly burst into tears
all over again. What had happened to the brother who had
promised to look after me? The fact that he had said he
never had time to reply to my letters should have warned
me that our closeness had broken down. I just couldn't
bear to admit it to myself.

"Can Suckley be that bad, sister?" Richard asked now.
"He has money, Arabella says. I know he's not a young
man, but surely some security and a high position would
be pleasing to you?"

At first I couldn't believe what I was hearing. Then I
almost slapped him. "How dare you listen to Arabella
when you have barely spoken to me? Has she told you that
Suckley is a liar and a lecher and a fool? Because that's
what she told me." Tears started in my eyes. "For the sake
of God, Richard! Don't you understand that Arabella only
cares about herself?"

Richard looked puzzled. "How could Arabella benefit
from your marriage? She is only concerned about your
happiness. Like all of us."

"All of us?" I shouted. "Have you been talking to our guardians behind my back?"

I imagined Arabella's wheedling voice. *"The sweet girl. She's as innocent as a child. At the very least, Suckley will look after her."*

A window opened above and I saw Hetty's face. She looked down and tipped the contents of a piss pot on to the gravelled path.

I led Richard away from the house and told him what Meg had heard, the morning of Lord Suckley's visit. That somehow our mother had a hold over our guardians, though the truth was that neither of them wanted me to marry Suckley. "Aunt Frances even told me our mother would make a dangerous enemy to you as well as them," I said to Richard. "Don't you see, it's not Suckley who's behind this marriage, it's our mother. But why? Why would she choose Suckley? I know he's rich, but so are lots of other men and most of them aren't pigs! Even Uncle Charles called him a 'mannerless oaf'."

Richard chewed his lip, frowning. "I think you are putting a lot of store on tittle-tattle from a child. Even so, I can't explain what Uncle Charles said to you. The truth is, I can't stop our mother from forcing this marriage on you. I have no influence and no money — and she has both."

"It's not about money, Richard," I cried. "It's about my life! I want you to write to her for me. For all I know, she thinks I'm bored with life in the country and she's doing

85

me a favour by marrying me off to someone, anyone, who will take me away from here. Although, in truth I don't think she cares about me at all."

"What good would writing to her do?" asked Richard. His eyes took on a pleading look and I knew he was going to make more excuses for himself. "Whatever her reason, she's made up her mind." He looked away. "The fact is, sister, Aunt Frances is right. Mother *would* make a bad enemy. Henry of Orgon has influence with the Queen and one word from him would put an end to my trade and I'd never have a chance to make my fortune." He reached out and touched my arm. "I don't want to end my days as a penniless sea dog."

"And I don't want to end mine with nothing to remember but a dirty old man crawling all over me."

"Emerald!" Richard's voice was shocked. "Don't speak like a fishwife!"

I stared at him. "I speak like Arabella," I said in an icy voice.

"How dare you insult Arabella!" snapped Richard. "She's been your true friend."

I felt my cheeks go hot. "Have you gone mad? Arabella has tormented me ever since we came to this house. You've barely seen her for seven years. You know nothing about Arabella!" The words were clamouring at my lips. *Arabella's pregnant. She wants to foist Suckley's bastard on you.*

I looked into Richard's face. Where before I had seen a kind, thoughtful man, now I saw a pathetic, foolish one.

His beard hid a weak chin, and his dark eyes had the idiotic, trusting look of a spaniel. I kicked up a clod of earth and splattered his clean hose.

"You fool!" I shouted. "You stupid, *stupid* fool!"

Molly whinnied the moment I walked into the gloomy stable. I filled up my apron with apples from the barrel and called back to her. Molly whinnied again, more loudly this time, and Richard's white gelding Merlin called back. Merlin was a difficult, stubborn animal and I had never liked him. Even so, I gave him an apple from my apron. It wasn't fair to take out my anger with Richard on his horse. Tethered to a ring beside him was a mare with a white flash on her nose and a gentle, patient look about her. I didn't know her, so she could only be Sam's horse. As I looked at her, I thought of Sam and the closeness of his body as we danced, the warmth of his breath on my ear. I longed for him to hold me again and the feeling was as painful as a bruise.

Molly whinnied once more and I lifted the bar from her door. As soon as I sat down on the wooden stool, she pushed her sticky, wet snout into my hands and I breathed in her sharp, rank smell and, little by little, the ache seemed to go away.

I thought of the time, almost a year ago, when I had first taken Molly on a rope through the meadows down to the river. Even though Tom had told me not to, I let her off the lead and watched as she waded in and gulped great mouthfuls of water like her mother would have done in some Bavarian forest before she was caught in a snare and shipped over to the bear pits in London.

It was thinking of Molly's mother that did it. Even though she had been a wild animal, I was sure she had had more kindness in her than the woman whose child I was. Suddenly all the hurt and disappointment I had felt since Richard's return crashed over me and I felt my chest go tight and my eyes fill with a million tears.

It had never occurred to me that my conversation with Richard would go so badly. Now I knew that if Arabella was determined to get her hooks into him, he was too weak and stupid to see through her. And appealing to Arabella's sense of honour was a waste of time. She needed a husband and Richard was available. As for me, the thought of Suckley pulling up my shift in the dark made me double over in despair.

I put my head in my hands and sobbed.

I don't know how long Sam had been standing there, but when I looked up he knelt beside me and held out a handkerchief. Later, it struck me that Molly hadn't growled.

"Come with me," he said gently. "You need some air." He pulled me to my feet and put his arm through mine.

We walked to the riverside and sat on the bank just a few feet from where I had caught the pike. By the time I had finished talking, Sam's handkerchief was sodden. The only thing I couldn't bring myself to tell him was the reason why Arabella wanted to marry Richard. It was such a filthy thing and he didn't have to know it.

I looked down at the handkerchief I was twisting round and round my fingers. "I can't marry Suckley, Sam. I'd rather join a convent and tell Tom to shoot Molly."

In my mind I saw Molly tied to a stake as Tom lifted his gun and pointed it at her. She was screaming with terror and her eyes were full of confusion. Then Tom pulled the trigger and she slumped to the ground. I began to cry all over again.

I expected Sam to say all the usual stuff about making the best of an arranged marriage given my circumstances, but instead he sighed heavily and spread his fingers.

I said, "It's not your concern. I shouldn't have worried you." As I spoke, I looked at his fingers. They were long and slender, almost more like a woman's than a man's. I wanted to reach out and touch them and the thought of those same fingers stroking my neck and moving lightly over my breasts made my cheeks turn scarlet.

To my horror, I groaned out loud and quickly turned towards the river so that Sam could not see my face.

"See that, uh, spit of stones?" I stammered. "That's where I landed the pike." I waited for the tremble to leave my voice. It was clear Sam was uncomfortable, and now I worried I had been indiscreet and compromised his friendship with Richard. "Please forget what I've told you. I was upset. It's nothing to do with you." The words sounded so false I didn't know what to do with myself.

"That's where you're wrong, I'm afraid," said Sam, in a voice that took me by surprise with its seriousness. "I am here because I came especially to meet you."

"*What*?"

I must have looked like a proper dolt because Sam smiled despite himself.

"I am telling you the truth," he said, putting away his smile. "Certain people have asked me to find out if you are prepared to help us."

"What do you mean, 'us'?" I had no idea what he was talking about. "Don't make fun of me, Sam."

Sam's face went still and he seemed more handsome than ever to me. "I'm not making fun of you, Emerald. Have you heard of Sir Francis Walsingham?"

I frowned. "He's a minister of the Queen."

"That's right," said Sam. "He's her Secretary of State, but he's also her spymaster. His work is to protect the Queen from danger."

I knew enough from conversations with my uncle that our Queen had enemies and that many of the powerful Catholic lords would be happy to see her dead.

I stared at Sam. "Are you telling me you spy for Walsingham?"

Sam held my gaze. "From time to time, I have a certain arrangement with him," he said. "The truth is, Emerald, that I am here on the Queen's business. Before I can say any more, you must swear to keep what I tell you absolutely secret."

The frothy sound of the river turned into a great roar. I felt as if my head was full of water.

I held up my hand and solemnly swore that I would keep secret everything Sam told me. He began to speak.

"Last November, I was a gentleman on the ship of war, *The Gloriana,*" he said. "We were crossing the Bay of Biscay when a storm blew up and we came across a French privateer that had lost her mainmast. Our orders were to patrol the coast and take any foreign ship we could, so we boarded the privateer and overpowered her crew.

"When I was sent below to arrest the captain, I found him in his cabin, stuffing a bag of documents out of the porthole. I knocked him out before he could finish the job.

"I sat down and read the documents straight away," Sam continued, his eyes holding mine. "And I found I was reading about a plot to poison the Queen while she was away from her Court this summer. No names were mentioned. The documents revealed only that the plotters are known to her but that she won't suspect them."

I was shocked, but still more confused than anything. I frowned. "I'm sorry. I don't understand how I could possibly help you."

Then I remembered Arabella telling me that it was my mother who had engineered the Queen's invitation to Bleathwood.

"Are you suggesting my *mother* is part of this plot?" I asked.

Sam shook his head. "It's more likely that Henry of Orgon is involved. But we have no evidence against him."

I looked up at him. "Both Richard and Arabella have told me he's trusted by the Queen."

Sam pulled a face. "They all are until they turn out to be traitors."

He picked up a blade of grass and split it with his thumbnail. "The point is that Lord Suckley is well known for his French sympathies and he may have become involved with extreme Catholics who believe they have a lawful right to kill a tyrant."

"Suckley?" I asked in a puzzled voice. "I would have thought he was too stupid to be a traitor. Besides, our Queen is not a tyrant."

"Of course she's not," said Sam. "But not everyone would agree with you and the belief in that right is enough for some men to justify killing her."

He dropped the bits of grass on the ground. "When Richard told me about your marriage, I had an idea that you might be prepared to help us with information about Suckley."

"Not if it means marrying him," I said shortly.

"All you need to do is cooperate with Suckley when you arrive at Bleathwood," said Sam patiently. "And remember who he talks to and what they say." He paused. "With your memory, that should be easy."

"I would do anything for the Queen," I replied. "But I

92

know nothing about Suckley's companions apart from the one that came here with him."

"What was his name?" asked Sam.

"Pierre Marchand," I said. The Frenchman's cold, baby face floated in front of my eyes. "He asked lots of questions."

"Tell me about him," said Sam.

I described how Marchand had called himself a perfumier and that he had spoken to every member of staff in the house in the space of two days. "I remember thinking he was an unlikely companion for Suckley."

"What do you mean?"

"By comparison, Suckley was a graceless, foul-mouthed runt."

Sam smiled. "I can see he lived up to expectations. Did you speak to Marchand on your own?"

I nodded. "He knows his herbs. Aunt Frances thinks he's taken work as an apothecary." I wondered if I should tell Sam that I had found something disturbing about the Frenchman, or whether he would think I was being childish. But I didn't have to decide.

"What is it about him that upsets you?" he asked.

I blushed despite myself. "How did you know?"

"I have learned to hear what people say even when they don't know they are saying it," said Sam. "I'll teach you, if you like. Though I suspect you won't need as many lessons as I did."

So I told him everything I could about Marchand,

from the moment I had first heard his voice, playing the game I used to play with Richard when we were children. "See how observant you are," said Sam, in a voice that was half playful and half serious. "You don't need any lessons from me."

Somehow we had moved closer together and I almost touched his hand as I spoke.

"I still don't understand what use I can be to you," I said. "I'm not as clever as you think I am."

I felt Sam shift towards me then pull back with an effort.

He let out a long breath and when he spoke again, his voice had changed and become serious.

"Listen, Emerald," he said. "Helping me is your only chance. To do it properly, I want you to become a Court lady. And that means wearing the richest gowns that can be had, not borrowed dresses from your guardian."

I blushed.

"I don't mean to insult you," said Sam quickly. "It is only because I look at you with the Queen's eyes, and indeed the Court's eyes, and I want all of them to notice you at Bleathwood. You must look the part for two reasons: so that you are fully accepted as a courtier and can then pass me any information you come across; and so that when the Queen sees your beauty and breeding, there's a chance she might question the suitability of your marriage."

Sam paused and said, "Walsingham will pay for your dresses and I will arrange it so that nothing looks

94

suspicious. In return for your help, I'll put in a word with him." He touched my hand. "Even if the Queen doesn't interfere herself, I'll ask him to persuade her that you and Suckley are ill-matched. Whatever happens, we will set you free."

I looked down at the grass. I didn't want to meet his eyes in case he saw the longing in mine. "So Richard couldn't have stopped this marriage?"

Sam split another blade of grass and scrunched it up in his fingers. "Richard couldn't have done anything for you. Something much bigger is going on."

"What do you mean?"

Now Sam looked uncomfortable. He said, "When I told you we believed your mother wasn't involved, that wasn't quite true. It was she who sought Suckley out, only two months ago. Your stepfather had nothing to do with it. But why Suckley? That is what is puzzling Walsingham and his men. Suckley has nothing in his favour yet she is prepared to give him her only daughter. There must be a reason."

A chill feeling went through me and I felt the hair prickle on the back of my neck. "Did you make friends with Richard just so you could meet me?"

"Remember everything we say is to be kept secret," replied Sam in a low voice.

I nodded and waited to see if he would tell me the truth.

"You know the answer already," said Sam. "As soon as

Walsingham's men found out about Suckley, someone had to meet with you. I was the obvious choice because I knew Richard from our time on *The Pigeon*."

Sam sighed. "Your brother is a good man, Emerald, and I have grown fond of him. Would it be so terrible if he married Arabella?"

"It would be wholly wicked."

We sat in silence for a few moments. So much had been said that both of us needed to let things settle.

"I am offering you the only chance you have," said Sam at last.

I looked into his violet eyes and I thought I would drown in them. "Then I would be a fool not to take it."

Sam took my hand. "Trust me," was all he said.

Chapter Seven

"Richard tells me you have decided to see sense about your marriage," said Arabella. It was a cold, damp evening a week later. Since Richard's arrival, Arabella had taken to wearing pale-coloured shawls and softly pleated wool dresses in pinks and blues. Even the cap she wore was lacy and girlish. Normally it was black. I could hardly bring myself to look at her.

The sympathy I'd felt for Arabella when she told me about Suckley had gone. Now all that remained was disgust. I hated to see her hanging on Richard's every word, and their hand-clutching made me want to throw a bucket of cold water over them.

"Richard should know better than to repeat private conversations," I replied. "Besides, I said nothing of the sort."

"Perhaps something has made you change your mind." Arabella arched her eyebrows and gave me a conspiratorial look. "I wonder if it has anything to do with the persuasive powers of Viscount Pemberton." She picked up the taffeta collar she was embroidering. "If you want my advice, don't trust him."

Even though I knew Arabella was still cross at Sam's indifference, I could see she was choosing her words carefully.

"I thought you had never met him before," I said.

Arabella shrugged her shoulders. "He has a reputation at Court for making friends easily and losing them as fast."

"Richard counts him as a friend," I said.

"Richard is a sweet, simple soul," said Arabella, with a knowing smile which was meant to tell me she knew more about my brother than I did. "He would befriend anyone who needed a favour."

"That's rubbish," I said angrily. Then I could have kicked myself. Arabella would know nothing about Sam and Richard, but now she might suspect I did. I changed the subject to stop her asking questions.

"When will your belly show?"

She stared straight back at me and her face didn't move a muscle. "Oh, not for a month or so," she replied. "There's still time to get rid of it if I have to."

"Then what do you want with Richard?"

"I might keep it," said Arabella. She pulled a long, pink thread through the end of her needle. "Babies need fathers. So Richard's my insurance."

"You make me sick."

Arabella smiled, and I swear her teeth had grown points like a bat. "If you really want to save your brother from a fate worse than death," she said quietly, "keep away from Sam Pemberton. He's much more my kind and, with a clear field, I'd win him over."

"You witch!" I sat on my hands so I didn't pull off her cap and grab her hair.

Arabella shrugged. "You are a fool."

"That's what your father called me the other day," I replied. "It seems none of you have a very high opinion of me."

"My mother has the greatest regard for you," said Arabella. "She has told me so on many occasions." She twisted her garnet ring. "I believe she feels sorry for you."

Was it jealousy I heard in her voice? I thought of my conversation with Sam. If I was going to get the information about Suckley he needed, I had to have Arabella on my side. I had to stop being childish and start thinking like she did.

"I need your help," I said abruptly.

"Haven't we acted out this play before?" Arabella widened her eyes in mock amazement. "Perhaps not. Perhaps we really *were* friends for a time. But now a witch asks a fool, what trick is this?"

"It's not a trick." I took a breath and began to act a part I didn't even know I could play. "Arabella, listen to me. Why should we be enemies? It's stupid for us to keep on hurting each other."

Arabella cocked her head. "Perhaps you're not such a

fool after all." She sat back and folded her arms. "What do you want of me?"

"I want you to teach me how to behave like a lady." The words nearly choked me, but I made myself give her a pleading smile. "It has turned out as you said. I can't stop this marriage, so I might as well prepare myself for it."

Arabella narrowed her eyes. "What has Sam Pemberton been saying to you?"

"It has nothing to do with Sam Pemberton." I turned away so Arabella couldn't see my face, and made myself think of Molly's dead body lying in a pit behind the stables. Tears rolled down my cheeks and fell on my hands. Then I looked back at Arabella. In my mind, Tom was standing over Molly, covering her with earth. "Richard won't help me," I sobbed. "He was my only hope."

To my surprise, Arabella's face softened. She looked as pale and pasty as an unbaked bun. "It's not that Richard won't help you," she said. "He can't. The truth is, there is nothing he can do to stop your mother getting what she wants. Even my father has warned him of her ruthlessness. She would destroy him if he crossed her."

"My mother is a curse on us all," I cried, and for good measure, I gulped noisily and blew my nose.

It was enough to satisfy Arabella.

"Poor innocent," she said, sounding pleased by my tears. "You must try and understand. Your mother is not a witch. She's a woman of the world and when you learn to be one too, you'll understand her. Of course I'll help

100

you." Arabella ran her fingers over the worn cuffs of my sleeves. "There are worse things than having a rich old man for a husband."

She took a pack of cards from her pocket. "Now let's put this tedious embroidery away and I shall teach you how to play gleek."

Arabella fanned the cards in her hand and began to take out the twos and threes of each suit and lay them down on the table between us. "It's a three-handed game, and today the Queen plays with us." She patted her purse. "So what is it you must remember?"

"If she wins, you must pay her right away."

Arabella laughed out loud. "Of course! Sam Pemberton told you. Her Majesty will not have debtors at her table."

This Court talk seemed to light a great candle in Arabella's mind. Her eyes blazed and her smile was bright. As she slapped the cards down on the table, I found myself hoping against hope that Suckley would keep his side of their sordid bargain and persuade Henry of Orgon to get her back into Court.

But not before she taught me her tricks.

Like it or not, I needed her.

Two days later, Uncle Charles unexpectedly took Richard and Sam off on a hunting trip. The wet weather had cleared, and there was to be a stag hunt in the forests behind Conwy Castle.

As soon as they left, an odd sense of freedom filled the

house. Now that the men had gone, the women seemed relieved to be on their own. Even for me, it was a good time to be in the garden with Aunt Frances and think my own thoughts in peace. As I picked sprigs of thyme and rosemary and sage leaves for drying, I thought about Sam. Aunt Frances never once mentioned Suckley's name. It was as if there was an unspoken agreement that we would enjoy this time together; although somehow both of us knew it would never come again.

Even Hetty and Sarah were friendly towards each other. There was time to clean the silverplate and wash bedsheets that hadn't been changed in months.

In the evenings, Arabella called for a young lute player called Jack and, once again, she taught me how to dance. Sometimes Aunt Frances sat by the fire and watched us, keeping time with her feet. It seemed to me that she looked happier than I had seen her for a long time.

One night, Arabella decided she would show me how to dance the galliard. The steps were slow and measured, and very difficult to follow without appearing clumsy. I tried again and again to copy what Arabella was doing, but I felt like a carthorse. Eventually Aunt Frances stood up and took over as Arabella's partner.

"Watch me," she said. "You must listen to the music as you dance." It was exactly what Sam had said.

I stepped back into the shadows of the room and watched as my aunt moved up and down with the elegance of a swan making its way across a still lake. Arabella looked clumsy beside her: I could see she was annoyed with her mother's interference.

"You must teach Emerald, Mother," she said. "I had no idea you had such skill with the galliard."

Aunt Frances ignored the sharpness in her daughter's voice. She simply turned towards me and held out her arms. And we danced silently up and down the stone floor. When I looked up, Arabella had gone.

The next morning, the skies were full of purple clouds and the air was heavy. A storm was coming and everyone was hurrying around the house trying to get things done. Through the front door, I saw Aunt Frances standing in the courtyard, wrapped in a shawl with a long, shallow basket under her arm. She was speaking to Cook, who held four dead rabbits tied together with cord. Everything about Aunt Frances had changed from the night before. She looked strained and tired as if she had been awake half the night, and her skin was the colour of curds.

"Dear Aunt," I said, holding out my hand to touch her arm. "You seem unwell. Where are you going?"

She looked at me vaguely. "There's elderflower in the hedges," she said. "It's at its best and I want to make cordial for Arabella for when she returns to Court."

Cook looked up at the sky. "Rain before noon, mistress. I'd stay in if I was you."

But I could tell Aunt Frances was determined to pick the blossom while it was dry. Even though she had no reason to think that Arabella would be leaving soon, a rain storm would bruise the elderflower petals and there would be no cordial or wine for another year.

"I'll get a basket and come with you," I said.

"That would be kind." Aunt Frances' face brightened.

As I turned to go into the house, Arabella's voice came down from the window above like the harsh caw of a crow. "You can't go!" she shouted. She was still in her nightdress with a blanket wrapped round her shoulders. "We're playing dice this morning."

Aunt Frances' smile froze. "We will walk another time, dear," she said to me. "I upset Arabella last night and she has been trying so hard to be kind to you." She touched my hand. "I never thought you two would be friends."

I looked into my aunt's washed-out face, and I felt like a criminal. If she knew the truth of our friendship, I was sure it would kill her.

"*Emmmerrralld*!" Arabella's voice shrieked again.

"Wait until tomorrow, Aunt," I said. "I'll come with you then."

Aunt Frances shook her head. "Bruised blossom goes mouldy," she said. "I'll be back before it rains."

"Then I'll help you strip off the flowers." I kissed her cheek and ran back up the front steps.

"Of course, everyone cheats," said Arabella as she drained her mug of weak beer and stuffed a large piece of a round, white loaf in her mouth. "But only if they can get away with it. Look." She waggled her wrist in the air and rolled out a pair of sixes three times in a row.

"How did you do that?"

"When I first went to Court, I was silly enough to play with Lady Rochford. It wasn't until Amy Trevelyan showed me how to sew a silk pocket up my sleeve that I began to win my money back."

She took my finger and guided it under her cuff and up her sleeve. Sure enough, there was a small oblong pocket full of dice. This time, as I watched Arabella waggle her wrist, I saw her quickly scoop up her own dice and roll the original pair on to the table.

"I could never do that," I said, smiling at Arabella's hoot of delight as she played her trick again.

"Why not?" asked Arabella.

"I'd never be fast enough." This was the answer she wanted to hear.

Like she said, everyone cheats.

Arabella sat back in her chair and held up her empty mug at me with a sly look. "At last!" she cried. "You're becoming a Queen's lady! Now I shall teach you how to make a full curtsey to the Queen."

She stood up. As she held up her skirts and swept one leg in a half circle behind, a huge *crack!* of thunder exploded over the top of the Hall. A second later, we couldn't hear each other speak for the sound of hailstones crashing down on the cobbles. In my mind's eye, I saw Aunt Frances running for cover under the oak tree in the south field. She would be holding her apron over the basket to keep the blossom dry.

Thunder crashed again, and the hailstones turned into sleeting rain. "My mother will be soaked," said Arabella as she watched the water splatter on the cobbles and quickly form puddles. "I can't think what put it into her head to go picking blackberries when a storm was coming."

"She was picking elderflowers," I said, feeling my good mood fall apart. "They were for you."

Arabella looked at me blankly.

"The cordial you take back for the Queen," I said. "It's made from elderflowers. Blackberries come in September."

"It's still daft to go out when there's a storm coming," said Arabella in a sour voice. "Now. Pay attention to this curtsey. I'm good at it."

I wasn't interested in curtsies any more. I opened the door and called for Hetty. A gust of wind screamed through the yard, and something fell from the roof and smashed.

"What do you want Hetty for?" asked Arabella, straightening her back from her low curtsey.

"Yes, Miss Arabella?" Hetty stood at the door, deliberately not looking at me. Ever since I had thrown her out of my room in front of Sarah, she had done her best to ignore me.

"Get me my cloak and my heavy boots, Hetty," I said

firmly. "I'm going to find her ladyship." I turned to Arabella. "Will you come with me?"

Arabella shook her head. "I hate getting wet," she said.

There is a field beyond the orchard where the elderflower bushes grow more thickly in the hedges than anywhere else within walking distance of the Hall. In the middle of that field is an ancient oak tree with huge low branches. No one would keep dry in this rain, but at least the leaves would be some kind of shelter.

This was where I had expected to see Aunt Frances, as soaked as I was, but at least out of the worst of the storm. But she was nowhere to be seen.

At first I told myself that I must have missed her as she made her way back to the Hall. There was another path she could have taken but I would have seen her on it. I wiped the rain from my face and tried to ignore the fear that was crawling over me.

It was raining so hard that the hills had disappeared behind a veil of thick, grey mist. Even though I was wearing my sheepskin cloak, it was soaked through and I was wet to the skin.

Through the rain, I saw the white shape of a sheep hobbling across the field. Even from where I stood I could tell it had a broken leg. I stared at the sheep, knowing that a fox would have her during the night unless someone brought her into the fold. Then it occurred to me that if my aunt had seen the same thing, she would have thought just as I had. The difference was Aunt Frances always took a length of cord with her on her walks, and a makeshift halter for a sheep would be an easy thing to make.

I shook out my cloak and set off across the field.

The ewe didn't move as I came towards her. She was sitting in the mud, blank-eyed and exhausted and I could see the anklebone on her back left leg was badly swollen. Then I noticed a cord halter tied round her neck.

Fear prickled at the edges of my mind. I ran over the ridges, through the green blades of wheat towards the hedge. The grass was long there, and I knew a deep ditch ran along the side of the field. I didn't see the tree root half buried in the ground. I stumbled over it and fell full length, knocking the wind out of myself. Gasping for breath, I crawled the last few yards to the edge of the ditch on my hands and knees.

The rain was heavier than ever. When I fell, the hair had tumbled out of my cap and fallen over my eyes. I yanked it to one side with my muddy hands and saw my aunt lying at the bottom of the ditch, her right arm sticking out at a crazy angle to her body. It was broken for sure.

I couldn't move and when I opened my mouth to call her name, nothing came out. It was as if I had seized up with the shock of seeing her. I made myself make my legs work and slithered into the ditch beside her. She didn't move or speak. It wasn't until I got my arm round her shoulders and began to pull her out of the ditch that the pain of her broken arm made her cry out.

She opened her eyes, and they were wild, as if she didn't know who I was. Then her head slumped into my arms and I heard her say, "Thank God," before her eyes closed and her body went limp.

I hadn't realised until I was in the ditch beside her that my aunt was lying in a puddle of water. I tried to roll her in my cloak to keep her warm but the sheepskin was wet and cold so I wrapped my body round hers and pulled the cloak round us both.

I don't know how long we lay like that – probably no more than a few minutes. Then I heard Meg screaming my name and I shouted back, and there was her face looking over the edge of the ditch, and Tom Bounds' voice shouting down the field that help was on its way, and then Meg was in the ditch beside me.

"How did you know?" I cried. "How did you find us?" My aunt groaned as Meg wrapped her shawl round her.

"I was under the table," said Meg. "I heard you askin' Hetty for your cloak. When the mistress didn't come home and no sign of you neither, I got Tom."

"But how did you know where to look?"

Meg sniffed and wiped her nose with her sleeve. "Best blossom's in the lower field. We all knows that."

She put her hand on my aunt's forehead. "Mistress is hot," she whispered. She reached into her skirt and held out a small piece of bone. "It's my pig knuckle," she said.

"Ma gave it me against fever." She spat on the bone and wiped it clean before handing it to me. "I'll have it back when she's well again."

Men's voices called out from behind the hedge. Then two farmhands appeared above us. They were carrying a length of canvas fixed to two long poles. I heard Tom's voice shouting at them to hurry.

Meg watched with frightened eyes as I pushed the pig knuckle up inside my aunt's sleeve.

Her skin felt as if it was burning.

My aunt had taught me to set bones, and I'd helped her enough times. But I was shaking so much I was good for nothing. In the end, I sent for Tom to put my aunt's arm in a splint.

"Tom Bounds?" Arabella had shrieked when I told her. "My mother's not some woolly-arsed ewe! Send for the surgeon in Llandrod!"

"Stop talking like a fishwife," I snapped. "That surgeon's cack-handed. And even if we found him, he'd be days getting here. Tom's a good bone-setter and once he's done I can treat her fever."

"Fever?" The colour drained from Arabella's face. "Is she in danger?"

"There's always danger with fever," I said. "Tom will set her arm, and that's that."

But Arabella didn't seem to be listening. She paced back and forth, rubbing her hands over her face. "Oh dear

God, help me," she muttered. "This cannot happen." She turned. "Have you sent word to my father?"

I gave her a hard look. "Arabella," I said. "You're his daughter. *You* send for him."

Sarah came out of Aunt Frances' room. "Tom's done with the arm," she said quietly. "She needs to be in bed. I'll send Hetty for hot water and linen."

"Tell her to hurry," I said. "Is the fire banked up?"

Sarah nodded and left us.

I looked at Arabella. "Shall I tell Sarah to call you when we've settled your mother?"

Arabella shrugged. "What good would I be? I'm no nurse."

As I turned towards the bedroom, Arabella took my arm.

"Emerald." Her face was confused and full of lines. "Don't let my mother die."

I put my hand on hers. "Stay," I said gently. "You can help me and Sarah."

Arabella shook her head and walked away.

Aunt Frances lay on her bed with her arm strapped across her chest. Her face was pale and sweaty, but she didn't seem to be in any pain. As I began to unlace her boots, I realised I was glad that Arabella had refused to come with me. It was strange. Even though she was my aunt's daughter, somehow she would have seemed out of place.

"You'll mend a lot quicker when we get you under the

111

quilts," I said as I pulled off her muddy boots. "Is your arm comfortable?"

Aunt Frances nodded and barely winced as Sarah and I unlaced her damp clothes and got them off her. As we unbuttoned her sleeves, something hard fell out on to the floor.

Sarah picked it up and frowned. "What's *this*?"

"A piece of pig's knuckle," I replied.

"From Meg?"

I nodded, and Sarah shrugged then wiped my aunt's face with a damp cloth rinsed in lavender water. We dressed her in a clean, white nightgown and put her thickest lambswool shawl round her shoulders.

"Will you make the cordial for me?" asked my aunt in a small, anxious voice. "The elderflowers will only keep for a day or so."

"Of course I will," I said.

I didn't have the heart to tell her the elderflowers were lying in a puddle, and that her precious basket had blown away.

"Can you remember why you fell?"

"I tripped over the ewe," replied Aunt Frances. "I was leading her home – otherwise the fox would have got her. It thundered and she bolted between my legs and pulled me across the field. When I managed to stop her, it was raining so hard I didn't see the ditch, and I stepped into it."

I looked into my aunt's eyes. Her irises were the tiniest

of black dots, as if she had some kind of concussion. "Did you hit your head?"

Aunt Frances felt above her ear with her good hand and nodded.

I put my fingers on the place she had touched and felt a lump the size of a blackbird's egg. "If there's a bruise inside, it could swell," I said. "Shall Sarah fetch the apothecary?"

Aunt Frances shook her head. "If there's a bruise inside, a few leeches won't make any difference."

I propped her up, half sitting and half resting against her pillows, while Sarah tidied the room and gathered up her muddy clothes. "Shall I come back, Miss Emerald?"

"I'll stay with her. If you could find some dry clothes for Meg, I'd be grateful. She'll be hiding in the bakehouse, I'd say."

The door closed. I picked up a small pottery jug from a stand by the fire and poured out a cup of warm wine. My aunt's face looked ghostly with tiredness. "Drink this," I said, putting the cup to her lips. "It'll help you sleep."

She swallowed a couple of mouthfuls and fell back against her pillows. "Oh dear. I feel so foolish. Has a message been sent to Charles?"

"Arabella wrote straight away," I lied. "They'll be home as soon as they can."

She nodded and closed her eyes.

I went over to the window and looked out over the courtyard.

The storm had passed as quickly as it had come. Now the sky was bright blue, and the wet cobbles were steaming in the sun. I closed the open pane against the noise of the courtyard, then pulled back her curtains and let the daylight into the room.

Aunt Frances hated gloomy rooms. When she woke up, she would want to see sunlight beyond the honeysuckle which grew outside her window.

Someone tapped at the door. Meg was standing in the hallway with a bunch of roses in her hand. To my relief, she was wearing dry clothes. They belonged to Sarah by the size of them.

I went and wrapped my arms round her.

"Meg Catchpole," I said, "I owe you the biggest favour in the world."

Meg wriggled out of my arms. "You don't owe me nothing, miss," she said stoutly. "We's in this together. You an' me and Sarah. I said I'd look out for you and I did." She held out the roses. "I brought these for the mistress. Can I give them to her?"

I nodded. "Quietly, mind. She's almost asleep."

Meg tiptoed into the room. She looked like a drawing in a book of fairy tales. Sarah's jacket trailed on the floor behind her, and her stick legs looked oddly thick in woollen stockings that had been folded down to act like socks.

"'Strewth!" she murmured. Her eyes were as round as saucers as she stared about the bedroom. "I never been 'ere before," she whispered to me.

114

I tried to imagine seeing my aunt's room through Meg's eyes. It would have seemed like something out of a dream.

The walls were decorated with the same plasterwork as the formal rooms below and painted with yellow and turquoise fleurs-de-lys. The bed curtains were made of heavy cream silk. There was a huge fireplace and Turkey carpets hung on the walls, some woven with birds, others with animals and fishes. In one corner was a polished oak chest and in another, by the window, a carved chair with a footstool. It was a beautiful, peaceful room.

As Meg set down her flowers, my aunt opened her eyes and smiled. She held out her hand and Meg fell to her knees, clutching it to her chest as if the hand was some kind of wounded bird.

"You're a good lass," whispered my aunt. She turned away and closed her eyes.

"Come, Meg," I whispered.

In the passage-way, Meg slumped beside me and buried her head in my skirt. I wrapped her in my arms and rocked her like a baby.

"Don't let her die," she sobbed.

It was exactly what Arabella had said.

It was dark and Sarah was shaking me. Through my window, I could see a full moon in a black sky.

"Miss! Miss!" cried Sarah. "Wake up! You're to go to her ladyship right away!"

"Is she worse?" As I stumbled out of bed, I realised I was still wearing my day clothes. "Have you told Arabella?"

"No." Sarah put a candlestick in my hand. "She only wants to see you, miss. I've asked her twice."

I shook my head to clear my thoughts, but I was still groggy and confused. I must have been asleep for hours.

"Wait, Sarah. I can't think straight. Fetch me some water."

Sarah passed me a pitcher of water and I splashed my face. "Please, miss. Hurry," whispered Sarah urgently. "I don't want to leave her."

I wrapped my shawl round my shoulders and took the candle Sarah was offering me. "I don't understand, Sarah. Who is sitting with my aunt?"

"No one, miss," said Sarah. "You went to rest and sent Hetty to be with her, but she sent Hetty away. When I told her you were asleep, she said to let you be."

I remembered that I'd gone to the kitchen to get something to eat and found Hetty sulking because no one had called for her. It seemed foolish to make even more of an enemy of her, so I'd sent her upstairs. "Keep the fire going," I'd told her. "I'll be back in an hour." Then I'd gone to my room and climbed on to my bed. That was five hours ago.

I turned to Sarah as we ran down the corridor. "Have you been with her all this time?"

"Yes, miss, but she was asleep like a babe. Then—" Sarah gulped. "Well, I must have dozed off because the

116

next thing I knew, she was awake and wanted me to make her ready for you."

It was too late to ask Sarah what she meant.

I walked into my aunt's bedroom on my own.

The room was full of shadows and the smell of apple logs burning in the fire. To my surprise, the curtains were still open and a silver light from the moon shone on the floor.

Aunt Frances was sitting up in bed. Her eyes were closed, but I knew she was awake. Now I understood what Sarah had meant. She wasn't dressed in pale nightclothes any more. She wore a bright red shawl edged with dark red satin. It was gathered round her shoulders and held together with a round, gold brooch set with lapis lazuli.

Sarah had dressed her hair, because it was brushed gently back from her face and tucked into a pleated black silk cap. In the light from the candle flame, her face looked as white and smooth as marble.

As I drew near, she opened her eyes and patted her hand on the bed. "Ah, good," she said. "You are here. Sit with me."

I sat down beside her and took her hand. It was clammy and cold.

"Aunt Frances. What is ailing you?"

She held up her shawl as if she hadn't heard me. "Red is the colour that heals," she said. "Sometimes it brings peace when there is no hope left."

I opened my mouth to chide her. *What nonsense, Aunt! Soon we'll pick berries where the elderflowers grew.*

But I didn't speak. It was foolish. I had seen death in many faces, and I saw it again now.

"That's well," said Aunt Frances, reading my mind. "We both know I am going to die." She put her hand on mine. "Do you love me, Emerald?"

"You know I do."

"Did you love your father?"

"My father?" I said stupidly. "Of course I loved him. But I can hardly remember him."

Suddenly I had a memory of the touch of his fingers on my shoulder as he passed behind my chair. I shivered. "Why do you ask?"

I don't know what I was expecting to hear, but I will never forget what she said.

"Because I am afraid you won't forgive me."

A log tumbled in the fire and a spray of bright sparks flew in the air. In the light, there was a look on her face that I had never seen before. It was deeper than sorrow.

"It was agreed between them," she said at last.

I had to bend forward to hear her.

"What are you talking about, Aunt?"

"My husband and your mother," she replied. "Listen. Your mother Millicent was the daughter of a Bristol merchant called Edwyn Garway."

I frowned. My mother had always told us she came from Devon, where her parents were relations of the Duke of

118

Exeter. Not that that mattered now. I thought about what my aunt had said to me down by the river when I first learned of Suckley's proposal. Something about my mother being a dangerous enemy if I didn't do what she wanted.

At the time, I hadn't dared ask my aunt what she meant and, in truth, she had been in no mood to tell me. I had a feeling I was about to find out now; it was a nasty, frightening feeling.

"When did you meet my mother, Aunt?"

"The year before she gave birth to Arabella."

"Surely you mean Richard?"

"No, I mean Arabella. Arabella is your mother's daughter. Charles is her father."

I closed my eyes and felt my head going round in crazy circles, like a spinning top about to topple over.

"Listen," I heard her say. "Please listen. And forgive me if you can."

I sat in the darkness as Aunt Frances explained that Hawkstone Hall was inherited through her family line and had nothing to do with my Uncle Charles. When she was sure she couldn't have a child who would inherit her estate, she and my uncle were introduced to Edwyn Garway. The Bristol merchant had all the money in the world, but he didn't move in the right circles to meet the powerful families that he wanted to introduce to his beautiful, ambitious daughter, who was called Millicent.

I didn't know what to say or if I should say anything. In the end, I put hands over my face and just listened.

In return for having his child, my uncle offered my mother one hundred gold crowns if the baby was born strong and well but, as the pregnancy progressed, it turned out that my mother wasn't interested in the money. She would accept his offer on one condition only. She wanted an introduction to Charles' great friend – Stephen, Lord St John of Croft Amber.

As I listened, I felt my head dropping lower and lower on my chest.

My father was a man of almost fifty, happiest in the company of books and nature. He had no inclination to marry. He had a sister, Eleanor, who had a son, Thomas, who was his heir.

Yet within a year, Stephen, Lord St John had married Millicent Garway.

"We flew in the face of God," said Aunt Frances. "We believed what had happened would be a secret between your mother and us. Charles drew up a paper. Your mother signed it. When she married your father, we trusted her to keep silent. Since the moment Arabella was born, there has been nothing but sadness and shame in our lives. Don't ask me if your father ever discovered what had passed between his best friend and his wife. I cannot say."

Aunt Frances' voice was faint, but it sounded like a high-pitched scream. "Charles saw nothing of him after his marriage. He didn't have the courage to look into the face of the friend he'd betrayed. As for your mother, we came to think of her as a she-devil.

"Ten years ago, we received a letter from your father. He asked Charles to be guardian to you and Richard in the event of his death, no matter what the circumstances. Charles agreed immediately. It was the least we could do."

My aunt sighed. "Two years later, your father died unexpectedly."

The voice that came out of my throat didn't feel like mine. "Do you think my mother poisoned him?"

Aunt Frances' eyes were two dark holes in her face. "I can't swear that she didn't." She paused. "Your mother has no love in her. Your father knew that, and he was afraid for you and Richard."

I thought of the years that had passed with no word from my mother until the arrival of the letter. Knowing what I knew now, I was sure Lord Suckley must have been useful to her in some way, and that I was his reward.

Aunt Frances was reading my mind. "When Charles received her letter, he was disgusted. We both were. You are a child, not a pawn in a game."

She bowed her head and I felt she was forcing herself to speak. "When I followed you down to the river that time, I was half crazed. Your mother is blackmailing us. I should never have taken her part."

She felt for my hand and held it. Her fingers felt like twigs. "Charles fears for Arabella, but I fear for you."

No words came into my mind to soothe her. I didn't feel angry or betrayed. I felt numb and very tired. I thought of Arabella in her bedroom. This dreadful story was her

121

tragedy more than mine. "Arabella is still your daughter, Aunt," I said at last.

"Arabella is Millicent's daughter," replied my aunt. "And so are you… yet it is you I love as my own. Please forgive me, Emerald. I can't bear to die if you don't forgive me."

"Then you must tell Arabella the truth while you can."

Perhaps she didn't hear me, or perhaps she didn't want to hear. I'll never know.

"Stay with me," she whispered. "We'll wake up and listen to the birds like we used to when you were a child."

I woke with my aunt's hand on my cheek. Her fingers were warm, so I knew she wasn't dead. I opened my eyes and saw the most beautiful rosy orange dawn spreading across the sky. Outside the window, the air was full of birdsong.

Beside me, Aunt Frances stirred. "My dearest one," she whispered. "Call Sarah to fetch the priest."

Chapter Eight

Aunt Frances died in my uncle's arms three hours later. The priest was beside her and her soul was with God. Arabella sat on a chair by her father's side with her head buried in her hands, and Richard stood by her. The two men had ridden through the night and still wore their muddy clothes and boots.

I stayed by the window and watched the sun turn the shadowy fields into patches of yellow and green. I couldn't bring myself to stand with the others. I knew too many secrets and I felt alone and very sad.

I don't know what I would have done without Sarah. When I had left my aunt's side, she had been waiting for me outside the bedroom, sitting on the floor.

"Her ladyship needs a priest, Sarah."

"He's below."

After I had told Uncle Charles everything I could about what had happened to Aunt Frances and how the fever had taken hold of her, Sarah led me away into the garden and we had picked violets together. For a few minutes, we said nothing as we knelt on the damp earth. Then Sarah rocked back on her heels and took a deep, gulping breath.

"I don't know what to say to the master."

"What do you mean?"

"He thinks Arabella was with her ladyship all night. If I told him the truth now, he would think I was lying."

"Has Arabella said anything?"

"Not to me. But she knows what her father believes and she hasn't told him otherwise."

"Dear God."

Sarah looked at me. "Miss Emerald, I'm not a liar, but I want to do what's best for you. Shall I say the truth if I'm asked? Or would it be better to leave things as they are?"

I sat down on the grass and tried to make myself think straight. It was bad enough trying to come to terms with what Aunt Frances had told me without making things worse by lying to my uncle.

But if I told the truth, I would be calling Arabella a liar. If her father believed me, it would cause a terrible rift between them. Then again, if he believed Arabella had spent the night with her dying mother, he was likely to suspect that she knew the truth of her birth.

Suddenly my whole world was full of lies, and the only way I could help myself was to tell more of them. Sarah was right. We had to pretend Arabella was telling the truth, that she had stayed with her mother and, if anyone asked, we would say Aunt Frances had not called for me. Uncle Charles would have known that it was inconceivable that my aunt would have wanted both of us with her at the same time.

"Did anyone see me going into my aunt's bedroom?" I asked. "Where was Hetty?"

"With her mother in the kitchen," said Sarah. "She never came upstairs again after her ladyship sent her away."

"And when you came to fetch me?"

"Everyone had gone to bed."

"Who knew about the priest?"

"Only Meg. I sent her to fetch him."

I rubbed my hand over my face. I had to get my story straight before anyone started asking questions. If Aunt Frances had wanted to keep my visit secret, it followed that she wanted me to keep everything I had heard secret. But it was too late for that. She hadn't known about Arabella and Richard.

What I heard next made my blood freeze.

Arabella's voice came from the other side of the yew hedge. She sounded upset and tearful. "I spoke to my mother last night." There was a silence as if she was trying to get herself under control. "I knew it would be my last chance. *Our* last chance, my darling. She gave us her blessing to marry."

I could imagine Arabella standing with her head on Richard's shoulder and his hand on her hair.

"Arabella." Richard's voice was thick but hesitant. "Please understand—"

A skirt rustled, and Arabella's voice came from a different place. I guessed she had pulled away from him. "I *don't* understand," she cried out. "Must I stay a sister to you for ever?"

My stomach shrank inside me. I looked at Sarah. She was frowning.

Richard spoke as if he was gulping air. "Dearest one. Listen to me. I haven't had a chance to speak to you alone since we came back. *The Pigeon* is fitted and ready to sail. Word arrived at Conwy. I leave today."

"No!"

I could hear the terror in Arabella's voice. In another few weeks her belly would have swollen, and it would be too late for anything. But something else made my stomach turn over. If Richard was leaving, Sam was leaving, too. I fought to stop myself from crying out.

"Arabella, please!" pleaded Richard. "What's wrong? We can wait. I want to come back with pearls for your wedding dress and a gold band for your finger."

"Marry me now," said Arabella. I could hear she was trying to sound playful, but her voice cracked. "I don't care for jewels. I only want you."

As quickly as I could, I crawled away over the grass and round a laurel hedge. Then I threw up in my hands.

When their voices died away, Sarah came over to sit beside me.

"Did they hear me?" I spluttered, trying to wipe away the sticky strings of spit that hung from my mouth.

126

"No. They've gone." Sarah held out a clean cloth and helped me to my feet. "Come, no one will look for you in the winter room."

On the other side of hedge, there was a doorway into the Hall between the log store and the brewhouse. The door led down a short corridor to a small room with a fire with plain hangings on the walls. In the winter, when Uncle Charles was away hunting, Aunt Frances and I used to take our sewing there. Sometimes we put our sewing away, and Sarah brought candles and mugs of spiced ale and we played draughts on an ebony board. I let Sarah take my hand and I followed her.

As we walked quickly into the house, I wondered if Sarah had guessed that Arabella was pregnant and that the father couldn't be Richard. I was sure she had. Sarah worked in the laundry room, and Arabella was not the kind of person who would bother to disguise her smallclothes.

The back corridor was empty. A moment later, we were in the little room. Sarah put a rug over my knees. "Stay here," she said. "Try and sleep. I'll come for you when you're needed." Then she left and closed the door.

I slumped back in the chair and closed my eyes. I could feel Aunt Frances' presence in the room so strongly that it was as if she was sitting in her usual chair. I opened my eyes, sure that I would see her; but of course the chair was empty. Her sewing bag hung over its back, and the rug I had woven for her last birthday lay folded on the footstool.

127

The door opened and Sarah came in with a mug of hot ginger wine and some bread spread with curd cheese. "No one's about," she whispered. "Rest while you can."

I realised I hadn't eaten for almost a day. I ate the bread and cheese instantly. As soon as the food was inside me, the horrors of the night flooded back and I felt such sadness and loneliness I thought my heart would break. I curled up like a baby and the only comfort I could find was the thought of Sam's arms around me. Then I remembered he was leaving and despite everything we had talked about, I knew I might never see him again.

I rocked myself back and forth as I held the picture of his face in my mind. I had to tell him the truth. I loved him and I wanted to live the rest of my life with him. I swallowed the wine and fell asleep.

I woke up with a shock. I had no idea where I was. I could hear Aunt Frances' voice in my ears. *Emerald! Emerald!* But it was in my dream, and in my dream I couldn't reply.

Meg was standing in front of me, bringing with her the musty, sharp smell of the stables and the reek of cooking fat from the spit in the kitchen. Part of me wondered why she was here, but I didn't ask. The last of my dream and the sense of Aunt Frances faded and tears began to run down my cheeks.

"Ah, miss. Don't cry." Meg put a handkerchief into my hand. "Her ladyship is with the angels now."

I wiped my eyes, hearing the sounds of the Hall beyond

the oak door. Hetty was calling for clean rushes in a shrill, tired voice. A beer barrel clattered on the flagstones as the brewer rolled it across the hall.

Meg set down a jug of hot water, and put a napkin and a tiny bottle of lavender on the table beside me. She held out a square of mirror. "Sarah told me to bring this to you."

She pushed the mirror awkwardly into my hands and took out a comb and a freshly laundered cap from her apron pocket. "And these."

"Leave me be," I muttered, waving the napkin away.

"I'm only doing what I was told, miss," said Meg in a hurt voice. She dampened the napkin and shook some lavender drops over it. "You'll feel better for it."

I pressed the napkin to my face and breathed deeply. It was almost too hot to touch, but the lavender vapour spread through my head like a wonderful soothing mist. Slowly, I felt myself coming to life again.

Meg took back the cloth and squeezed it out in the jug. This time I rubbed it all over my face and neck, pulled off my cap and scrubbed at my head as if I was washing a muddy dog.

I handed her the napkin. "I'm sorry I snapped at you, Meg."

"No mind, miss." Meg smiled shyly. "As long as you're feeling better."

The door opened and Sarah walked in. Her face was grey and haggard, and there were black shadows under her eyes. But there was something determined and fierce about her.

Meg shrank away. "I done what you asked," she said defensively. "Don't you snap at me now."

"You've done well, Meg." Sarah held open the door. "Take the jug to the scullery. There's a hot meat pie for you in the kitchen."

Footsteps thudded up and down the big stairs in the hall. Somewhere beyond, we heard the steady tolling of the chapel bell.

"They're laying out the mistress," said Sarah, in a voice that was barely there.

"Not in the Great Chamber?" The Great Chamber was Uncle Charles' room. My aunt had never liked its ostentation.

Once, in the herb store, we had been talking about death. Aunt Frances had said quite firmly that she wanted to be laid out in her bedroom, not the Great Chamber. "Imagine lying in a box, looking up at that ceiling," she had said with a wry smile. "All those patterns and colours and coats of arms – I'd never get any rest." The ceiling in her bedroom was plain white plaster with a delicate stencil of ivy leaves that wound round the top of the walls.

"No, no," said Sarah. "Her ladyship is in her room. She told the priest, so no one can move her." She put a couple of logs on the embers of the fire. "Arabella is in charge."

"Does my uncle know the truth?"

Sarah shook her head. "Arabella told him her mother never called for you." She looked at me sadly. "I'm sorry, miss. I saw his face. It was what he wanted to hear."

"Have either of them asked for me?"

"No."

It was odd, but I didn't feel hurt or jealous. The woman I had loved as a mother was dead after a life of anguish and guilt. All I wanted for her was peace.

"What clothes will they dress her in?"

"Her best linen nightgown, and she's to be wrapped in the scarlet shawl," replied Sarah. "She told the priest what she wanted."

Sadness washed over me. My aunt would have known that only the priest could have overridden her husband or her daughter's wishes. And that they would have dressed her in her richest clothes and taken her down the stairs to lie in the Great Chamber, where she felt so uncomfortable.

"How does Arabella seem to you?"

"As if she were made out of stone. God knows what's in her mind." Sarah looked away. "I'm sorry, miss, I spoke out of turn."

"Why not?" I said. "You were a true friend to my aunt and you're the only friend I have. I'd trust you with my life."

Sarah looked at me hard. Then she held out a square of paper folded up in four. I knew who it was from before I opened it.

Please see me. S.P.

"He's waiting in the yard," said Sarah. "Will you see him?" She held my eyes as I picked up the comb.

"Yes."

Sarah smiled. "Give me the comb. You'll make a dog's dinner of yourself."

Sam came through the door in leather riding boots and a black wool doublet. His face was flushed and worried. It was all I could do not to jump up and throw my arms round him. I loved him, and every muscle in my body ached to hold him.

In one movement, he was beside me. "Where have you been? I've been looking for you everywhere."

I tried to speak, but I couldn't breathe and I couldn't stop myself trembling.

"Sweet Jesus," cried Sam. "What's happened to you, Emerald? What's wrong?" He took my hand and his fingers were warm and strong. I thought of Aunt Frances' cold, twig-like grasp and I thought I was going to cry.

"I have to talk to you," I said, clenching my other hand so tightly it hurt. "I know you're leaving so there isn't much time."

If Sam was surprised, he didn't show it.

I said, "Remember when we sat by the river and you made me swear to keep secret whatever you told me?"

"Yes."

"I need you to make me the same promise now."

132

"Emerald," Sam said. His hand tightened over mine.

"Don't say anything," I said in a choked voice. "Promise me."

"I promise," said Sam.

I looked up at his face and into his gentle, violet eyes and I told him everything.

I don't know what I was expecting Sam to say. When I finished talking, the relief of sharing all my dreadful secrets made me feel almost light-headed and I sat back in the still of the room and closed my eyes. Above the crackling fire the chapel bell tolled sadly.

"Christ's blood," said Sam at last. "You're sure your aunt was in her right mind?"

I nodded. "From what Sarah told me, she had thought everything out very carefully. No one saw either of us come or go."

"And Arabella? Are you sure she is carrying a child?"

"Why would she lie to me?" I asked. "She is pale as wax, and her morning breath stinks of sick. It was a gamble that didn't pay off." I shook my head. "It wouldn't matter except that now she intends to marry Richard."

"Suckley deserves her," muttered Sam.

"Perhaps. But what shall I do now? If I tell my uncle the truth, I call Arabella a liar. If he finds out it was me who sat up all night, he'll guess Aunt Frances told me that Arabella isn't her child."

Sam thought for a moment. "The point is that since Hawkstone is passed down the female line, Arabella only loses her right to inherit if the truth of her birth becomes known."

"Or if she has a bastard out of wedlock," I said.

"That wouldn't matter as far as Hawkstone is concerned," said Sam.

He looked at me.

"Do you think her father would force Suckley to marry her if he knew she was pregnant by him?" He smiled wryly. "That would certainly solve your problem."

The thought that Arabella could marry Suckley had never occurred to me. "I can't say what my uncle would do," I replied. "But I'm not telling him anything. Besides, if Suckley married Arabella, then what happens to my mother's plans for me?" I shook my head. "I suspect she would tell the truth about Arabella's birth just to spite them both. Then Suckley could refuse to marry her because her lineage is false and Arabella would be back where she started, but worse because she'd be an acknowledged bastard carrying a bastard herself."

"What an amazing mind you have," said Sam ruefully. "I have never met anyone like you."

I looked away to hide the blush on my cheeks. "The point is, what shall I do about Richard?" I asked. "I can't let Arabella trick him. But wretch that she is, I don't believe even she'd go through with it if she knew the truth." I turned back to him. "What *am* I going to do?"

For a moment, Sam didn't speak. Then he said, "There's no need to tell Richard anything right now, and for your own sake it is safer to keep what you know to yourself. There's no chance of Richard marrying anyone until we come back in August and by that time Arabella's belly will be obvious."

"How can you be sure?" I swallowed. "Richard is a weak man."

Sam smiled. "I'm sure because Richard and I intend to make our fortunes on this expedition. Then we have made a promise that when we return we will marry at the same time."

"You? Marry?" I heard myself squawk like a chicken. "Why didn't you tell me?"

"How could I?" asked Sam. "I have not asked my lady yet."

My mouth dropped open. Then I saw the gleam in his eyes.

"I love you, Emerald," said Sam, taking me in his arms. "I've loved you from the moment I saw you in the court-yard, hiding behind the doorway."

His mouth was on mine before I could speak, and I found myself kissing him back even though I had never been kissed by a man before. My lips parted and our tongues curled round each other, almost shyly at first then more urgently and insistent. I felt Sam's sighs become groans of desire as he moved his mouth on to my neck and over the swell of my breasts. I had never known such a feeling in my body before. Every part of me fizzed like a firework.

"Marry me, Emerald," Sam whispered at last. "Will you marry me?"

I pulled back from his kisses and buried my face against his chest. His wool doublet pricked my skin, but it could have been made of thorns for all I cared.

"Yes, I'll marry you," I whispered back. "I love you more than my life."

Sam took my face in his hands and kissed my forehead. "I will dream of you every night when I'm gone."

At the thought of him leaving, tears welled up in my eyes, and the happiness inside me began to shrink away to nothing.

Despite all our plans, Sam and I needed a miracle to be together.

"When will I see you again?" I asked.

Sam looked into my eyes and stroked my neck. "Our expedition takes us only to Spain. I will be back in Walsingham's service when the Queen arrives at Bleathwood."

I could hardly bring myself to ask. "What if you are too late?" I whispered.

"I won't be," said Sam firmly. "We will marry this summer. I promise you."

He lifted my face to his lips to kiss me, but I pulled away again.

"Wait." I untied the velvet bag I wore on a knotted cord around my waist and took out a key fixed to a silver ring. Then I crossed the room and lifted a small wooden box from inside a linen press. I fitted the key to the lock and took out the leather purse my father had given me in his writing room all those years ago at Croft Amber.

I handed Sam the purse. "Take this," I said, smiling. "I will be an investor before I am a wife." Tears were running down my cheeks, but I was happy again.

This was the moment my father knew would come to me. I threw my arms round Sam's neck and I kissed him hard like he had kissed me.

Chapter Nine

A few days after Sam left, I heard Aunt Frances call out my name in the middle of the night. Inside the cave of my bed hangings the air was full of her rose water scent, and I had the strongest feeling that she had been bending over me.

I sat up with a jolt and felt her disappear like a ripple on a still pond.

I had heard stories of the dead calling out to the living.

The old wives said it happened once, and then the dead one was gone for ever. I huddled under my quilt and felt for the gold locket Sam had given me the morning he left. Inside was a lock of hair and a piece of the caul that he was born in.

At first I had refused to take the locket – a sailor born in a caul never drowns, and I didn't want to take away his luck. But Sam told me that I was his luck now and it would be a precious secret, like the secret of our engagement.

Except that it wasn't a secret from Sarah. She told me later that she had knocked twice but neither of us had heard her. She had seen my flushed face and the locket around my neck and drawn her own conclusions.

She had come to tell us that Richard wanted to leave while the weather was dry. It was time for Sam to go, too.

"Come with me and say goodbye," Sam had said when Sarah left the room.

But I didn't want to speak to Richard. I could only think of him as a weak, foolish man, who had let me down when I had needed him most. And I worried that if Arabella was there, she would see in my face what had happened between Sam and me.

I shook my head. "If Richard had wanted to say goodbye, he would have asked for me."

Sam kissed my forehead. "Be strong, dearest," he whispered. "I will come back for you."

I clung to him for a moment and then I let him go. When the door shut behind him, I sobbed like a child.

Aunt Frances was buried in the chapel a few days later. There was no funeral procession. Her coffin was carried on the back of a cart. Even though Sarah and I had covered it with flowers, it was a sad, lonely sight. My uncle walked in front, staring ahead as if his face was made of hard clay. Arabella walked beside him. They didn't look at each other once and he never took her arm. It was as if they were separated by an invisible wall.

In the days after the funeral, I wandered through the

house, looking for a trace of the woman I had loved as a mother. It seemed impossible that someone who had been so strong and sure in her life could have left this world so completely.

I went to the herb store, where we had spent hours stripping lavender and filling round baskets with flower buds. It was here that my aunt had told me about the changes happening to my body, and why the bleeding that had begun in me was nothing to fear. And it was here that she had told me how different plants helped against sickness and how to recognise the signs of illness in other people's faces.

But when I stood in the room now, there was no sense of her at all. The herb store was nothing more than a tidy room hung with dried plants.

Without my aunt, the Hall stopped being a home, and became a shell of oak timbers filled with wattle and daub and sealed with plaster. My uncle spent his days in his study or hunting with his dogs. His face was grey and pouchy and when I spoke to him, all I saw was suspicion in his eyes.

I couldn't comfort Arabella and she said nothing to me. The lies that had been told and the harsh words that had been spoken since my aunt's death were too much for me to overcome and for the most part, I kept to myself and dreamed about Sam.

Once, when I was alone with my uncle, I almost asked him. Did he really believe that it had been Arabella who

140

had sat up all night with her mother and that Aunt Frances had never once called for me?

I am sure now that he must have known the truth. But it was impossible for me to ask. Arabella had already lied to him. It was too late for both of them.

Two weeks later, as Arabella had foretold, my mother's letter arrived, summoning us all to Bleathwood. My marriage was to take place during the Queen's summer visit.

I held the thick paper in my hand and let my eyes travel slowly over my mother's spiky writing. I owed Arabella a favour. If she hadn't warned me, I would have been in a terrible state. As for Arabella, with Richard's departure and no sign from Suckley of a return to Court, she was becoming more and more desperate.

When I came to the bottom of the letter, my stomach went cold.

It will be our pleasure to look after the bear until the Queen's arrival. I am sure Her Majesty will be grateful for your contribution to her entertainment.

I stared at the letter, hearing Suckley's thin, boastful voice in my ears. *A bear on a rope belongs in a pit.*

The wretch had told my mother about Molly.

I folded the letter carefully and put it inside my Bible. I had promised to be Sam's eyes and ears. It was the only chance we were going to get. But I had to think of a way to keep Molly away from the Queen.

* * *

141

Two weeks later, just before dawn, Sarah came into the room, with a jug of hot water in each hand. "Tom's waiting for you, miss."

I jumped out of bed and splashed my face with water. "Same place?"

Sarah nodded.

"Is anyone about?"

"No one that matters. "

Sarah handed me a ragged skirt and a jacket I kept hidden in the clothes chest. She took two wrinkled apples and a piece of bread from her apron pocket. "I'll meet you in the herb store."

I put the food in my pocket and smiled at her. "Thanks, Sarah. I couldn't do this without you."

Sarah smiled back. "And I couldn't do *anything* without you, miss."

I picked up my leather slippers and ran down the corridor in stockinged feet.

Tom was waiting with Molly under the oak tree in the south field. It wasn't far from the Hall, but no one could see it from any of the windows.

As soon as Molly saw me, she whinnied and pushed her nose into my jacket pocket. I took out one of the apples Sarah had given me and let her eat it from my hand.

"You should keep them apples as rewards, Miss Emerald," said Tom.

I pushed my fingers deep into Molly's fur and rubbed behind her ears. "Sorry, Tom. I always forget."

"Lucky I got others," replied Tom. "Now take this rope, miss, and lead her round in a circle. If we's going to learn this trick before you go, we needs every moment."

I took the braided rope from his hand and led Molly into the middle of the field.

It had been Meg's idea to teach Molly a few tricks before setting off for Bleathwood. "If Her Virginess finds out how clever Molly is, perhaps she won't eat her."

"The Queen's not called her 'Her Virginess', Meg. She's called 'Her Majesty' or 'Her Highness'. And she doesn't *eat* bears."

"Who cares?" said Meg. "She lets her *dogs* eat them. That's almost as bad." She pulled a face. "Maybe Her Virginess ain't as clever as they say she is."

"Just because she's cruel, it doesn't mean she's stupid," I replied. "She's supposed to be kind sometimes, too."

That was when the idea that a clever Queen might be kind to a clever bear began to take shape in my mind. And the only person who could help me was Tom. Molly had to learn tricks. If the Queen was amused, she might spare her life, and indeed give me a chance to live the life that I wanted with Sam.

"We'll teach her two things, Miss Emerald," Tom had said as soon as he heard my plan. "To do tumbles on the end of a rope and to let you ride her with a saddle on her back."

I shook my head. "I've never seen a bear let anything on its back except a monkey in a scarlet coat."

Tom grinned his gap-toothed grin. "Nor has the Queen."

He took down a child's saddle from the stable wall and held it in his hand. "This should be light enough."

The training began.

Over the next couple of weeks, Tom took Molly out every day and taught her how to turn somersaults on the end of a long rein. As it turned out, Molly was a natural performer and liked to learn tricks when there were rewards to be had. We taught her the tumbles first, and then the hard work began. Tom put the saddle on her back, strapped a sack of corn over the top and led her round again.

The first time I climbed on to Molly's back, I tried to sit side-saddle, but she reared up and threw me off. That was when I realised that I would have to wear breeches if I was going to have a chance of staying on.

So Sarah found me a pair of breeches and, day after day, I climbed on to Molly's back. And each time she threw me off. Finally, I went against Tom's advice and rode her bareback, holding on to the rolls of loose skin around her neck.

Perhaps it was what Molly had wanted all along. After that, she never threw me off again.

Now all I had to do was get a costume. It wouldn't do to appear in front of the Queen dressed in hand-me-down clothes. I thought of the monkey in its scarlet coat with the gold braid. If I had to wear breeches, then why not make them out of scarlet satin sewn with gold braid and a jacket to match? To avoid scandal, I could wear a velvet hat to hide my hair, and a mask over my eyes to disguise my face.

When I explained my idea to Sarah, she clapped her hands with delight. She was a talented seamstress and since everyone in the Hall knew that she was coming with me to Bleathwood, no one questioned the hours she spent in my room, sewing by the window.

One morning after I had come back from the field with Molly, I went to the herb store. It was here that Sarah waited with clothes for me to change into so no one would see me in my boots and breeches.

"Arabella has been calling for you since first thing this morning," said Sarah, handing me my petticoat and kirtle. "It was all I could do to stop her looking for you in the stables."

I unbuttoned the breeches and dressed in my own clothes as quickly as I could. "She didn't find out about Molly, did she?"

"Of course not," replied Sarah. "But something's up with her. She's as white and jittery as a goose."

We exchanged a look and, once again, I wondered what she knew.

In truth, I didn't know what to think of Arabella any more. In the weeks that had passed, seeing her sitting on her own, pretending to write letters, I had stopped hating her like I did when my aunt died and Richard left.

It wasn't her fault that she was my mother's child and that the woman she had believed was her mother had never been able to love her. Sometimes I wondered whether it would be better for her to know the truth of her birth. It might even come as a relief to her. Almost nothing could be worse than the situation she was in.

There was no reply from Arabella's bedroom when I knocked so I went out into the courtyard and called her name.

Hetty's head appeared from the bedroom window above me. There was something black and shiny in her hands. I guessed that she had been trying on Arabella's clothes. "Where 'ave you bin?" she demanded rudely. "The mistress bin askin' and askin'."

Hetty had taken to calling Arabella "the mistress" ever since Aunt Frances had died. Doubtless it made her feel more important; but it made me furious, and she knew it. My fingers tightened round the apple core in my hand. "Where is she?"

"Gone to the village," said Hetty.

"When did she leave?"

Hetty stuck her head out of the window again. "How should I know?" she snapped. "I ain't her keeper."

There was a startled squawk as the apple core hit her on the nose.

146

"I'll tell the mistress!" spluttered Hetty as she wiped bits of apple off her face. "You ain't nothing in this house any more. You'll be sorry."

"No, Hetty," I said. "*You'll* be sorry when I tell Arabella you're straight into her clothes press the moment she leaves her chamber."

The path to the village ran through a field of sheep and over a stile beside a field of barley. Then it forked two ways. One way led straight through a meadow of daisies and down on to the village. The other path went left into the birch-tree wood where Ma Wipeweed lived. It was well over a month since Arabella had told me she was pregnant. I turned left and began to run.

I found Arabella bent double behind a hedge, puking up a stream of yellow bile flecked with blood. Her hair hung in stinking wet strings from her face and her clothes were covered in vomit.

"Emerald!" she moaned. "Sweet Jesus!" She groaned and buried her head in her hands.

"When did you drink it?" I shouted. "*When?*"

Arabella shuddered and vomited again. "I don't know. An hour ago? I don't know."

I put my hands under Arabella's armpits and dragged her upright so she could lean on my shoulder. Our village was no different from any other, and even bushes had eyes. I had to hide her before someone saw us.

147

The only place to go was back to Ma Wipeweed's hut. It was the nearest and Arabella would be safe from prying eyes there. I was certain the old witch would run off the moment she saw us coming. Then once I'd got Arabella safely inside, I'd have time to think what to do next.

Five minutes later, I kicked open the wooden door. Sure enough the hut was empty, but the stink of it was worse than a dead rat. In the fetid gloom, I saw a cauldron hung over a low fire. A chipped bowl with a crust of green sludge sat on a plank. Beside it a jug dripped a lumpy, grey liquid on to the floor. I looked around to see if I could find a bucket. To my relief, there was one under the table and it looked as if it was full of water.

In the corner was a pile of dirty straw covered with sacking. I heaved Arabella on to it and tried to pull the sacking over her to keep her warm. As I grabbed the edges, the cloth came apart in my hands, and hundreds of black bugs scuttled out from underneath and disappeared into the mud walls.

Arabella was beginning to shudder. I looked around for something to cover her with, but there was nothing. So I took off my kirtle and wrapped her in that. Then I dipped a piece of my petticoat in the water and began to wipe her face.

I had never seen anyone look so sick in my life. She was panting more than breathing, and her skin was a chalky-yellow, as if her liver had gone bad. She groaned and I held her head while she vomited. She was sick so many times that there could not have been anything left inside her.

148

"Leave me," said Arabella at last, turning her head. "Let me die here."

"You aren't going to die," I said, as I wiped her face again. "Lucky for you, you puked everything up."

I smoothed back her sticky hair over her forehead and tried to make her comfortable on the pile of filthy straw.

Arabella turned her head to the wall and howled like a sick dog. "I can't go on any more."

There was such misery in her voice, I felt tears come to my eyes. At that moment, I decided to tell her the truth. After that, nothing else could hurt her – and it might stop her from destroying her own life as well as Richard's.

I moved close beside her so our bodies were touching and took her hand. "Arabella," I whispered. "Listen to me."

At that moment, the door opened and I saw the outline of Sarah standing against the light. At first she didn't see us then her eyes got used to the gloom. "Jesu," she muttered. "I thought as much." She looked at the dripping jug and the bowl crusted with the green sludge of chopped hay. "Has she been sick?"

"Yes."

Sarah bent over Arabella and peered into her face. "She'll live. Can she speak?"

I nodded and warned her with my eyes to pick her words carefully. "But how can we get her back without anyone seeing her?"

Sarah made the tiniest movement of her head to show

149

she'd understood. "They'll see her, all right," she said. She took off her shawl and wrapped it round Arabella's shoulders. "Only they won't know what they're looking at. Leave it to me."

Chapter Ten

A few hours later, Arabella and I climbed up the back stairs in silence. Our petticoats were dripping and our hair was stuck to our heads. We were both soaked to the skin.

Sarah's tale was the talk of the Hall. She had gone to look for wild strawberries when she'd heard me arguing with Arabella by the river. *Just like two cats*, she told Cook. So she crept nearer to hear what we were saying and that was when she saw me grab Arabella by her jacket and pull her towards the bank. Next thing, we had both stumbled over a dead branch and fallen headlong into the water. Sarah said she'd never heard such howling and poor Arabella must have hit her head because when she managed to clamber out, she was all groggy and her eyes were red and bruised. It was a miracle neither of us had drowned.

At the time, I thought Sarah's idea was a stroke of genius. We couldn't have smuggled Arabella up to her room without being seen. The only way had been to make a real show of it and, at the same time, wash the puke from her dress and explain her swollen eyes.

What I hadn't bargained for was the response from Uncle Charles.

"Wretch!" he yelled at me as he strode out of the back porch towards us. "How dare you behave like a jealous child?" He tried to put his arm round Arabella's shoulders, but she ducked away from him.

"It was an accident, Father," said Arabella with as much strength as she could. "Stop shouting like a madman."

"We stumbled, Uncle," I said. "I didn't mean for us to fall into the water."

My uncle wasn't listening. "How dare you risk Arabella's life?" he yelled. "I should never have taken you into my house. All you've brought us is trouble!"

I stepped back as if he had slapped me. But before I could say anything, Arabella turned to her father and snapped, "That's a lie and you know it. Mother loved Emerald. Not me."

"Nonsense, Arabella! Of course your mother loved you!" My uncle tried to pull her towards him, but she pushed him away.

"Don't tell me what is nonsense," said Arabella. "I know the truth!"

My uncle stood stock still. "What truth do you know?" he asked.

I turned away. One look at my face would tell him everything.

"I know that Emerald was the daughter my mother wanted," cried Arabella. "I might have been a changeling for all she cared about me."

My head went cold and for one terrible second, I thought I was going to faint.

My uncle's fury saved me. He turned and glared at me, and the veins on his forehead bulged like worms. "You deceitful little snake!" he yelled. "You stole a mother's love. You should be ashamed!"

"An' she's no right to order me about," called Hetty from the back, sensing that she could get away with it.

She turned to Arabella. "I've laid a fire in your room," she said sweetly. "And there's steaming water for your bath."

Arabella ignored her. "What mad fancy is this?" she asked her father in a furious voice. "Emerald stole nothing from me because there was nothing to steal. We both know that."

"Watch your tongue, Arabella!" yelled my uncle. He pushed her roughly towards Hetty. "Now go, before you catch your death! I'll not lose my daughter and my wife within a month."

He turned on his heel then stopped and looked back at me. "And you," he snarled, "stay out of my way."

I met his eyes and held them. He was a coward and a liar and I would never trust him again.

"I'm sorry, miss." Sarah came up to me with a blanket in her arms. "This is all because of me."

153

"I couldn't have left her, Sarah."

"No, miss. But I doubt she would have done the same for you." She put the blanket round my shoulders. "Such horrible words," she said under her breath. "He'll be ashamed."

I pulled the blanket closely round me. The sooner I told Arabella the truth, the better.

Arabella was lying in her bed staring at the fire when I tapped at the door and walked into her room. She didn't move or say a word as I sat down on the pale green satin quilt Aunt Frances had sewn for her eighteenth birthday. It was embroidered with rosebuds and lined with rabbit fur. Aunt Frances had promised me one like it when I turned eighteen.

I reached out to take Arabella's hand. Then I pulled back. She had never wanted sympathy in her life. Why would she start now?

"I know you were with my mother when she died," Arabella said in a dull voice. "I had it all worked out. Two birds with one stone. My father's respect and Richard as a husband and all for one lie I knew you would keep secret."

A log crashed in the fire and threw up a spray of yellow sparks that gleamed on the wet floor where the bath had stood. For the first time, I was aware of the fragrance in the room. It was Aunt Frances' rose-petal oil. She always put it in her bathwater.

154

It was odd. I had thought it would be easy to tell Arabella what her mother had told me. After all the dreadful lies, I was sure that the truth would somehow be healing, that it might even be a new start for both of us. But as soon as I tried to speak, I began to shake as if I had the palsy.

Arabella frowned. "Emerald," she said. "What's wrong? Are you sick?"

The sound of her voice made me shake even more. I tried to speak again, but all I could do was gasp for air as if I was choking. Nothing could make the words form in my mouth. I rubbed my hands back and forth over my face and heard Aunt Frances' voice in my head. *I can't bear to die if you don't forgive me.*

"Arabella needs a chance, too," I muttered. It was madness. I was talking to a dead woman.

Arabella's face went grey. "Who are you talking to?" she asked. "What's this about 'a chance'?"

I breathed deeply. I didn't know where to start; so I began at the beginning – at the moment I had walked into my aunt's shadowy bedroom and seen her sitting up in bed wrapped in her finest red wool shawl, pinned with the lapis lazuli brooch. I told Arabella everything her mother had told me that night.

When I had finished, we sat in silence. Then Arabella said in a tiny voice, "Does anyone else know this?"

I wanted to be as truthful as I could without mentioning Sam. "I'd say Sarah suspects you are carrying a child, but Richard knows nothing." I shrugged. "What business is it of his?"

Arabella managed the smallest smile. "I'm glad you see it that way. I don't deserve your generosity." She spread her fingers. "This is the oddest puzzle. We are half-sisters, but no one need ever know." She looked me straight in the face. "Is that how you see it?"

I nodded and held her gaze. "But I'll never forgive what your father did to mine. He knew our mother was determined to marry him." I found myself shaking as I remembered my father's absent, elderly ways. "He didn't stand a chance against her."

"Seems I've got bad blood on both sides." Arabella tried to look rueful, but it didn't work. Her face was full of misery. "Tell me the truth, Emerald. Am I really like her?"

It was a difficult question to answer. I hadn't seen my mother for such a long time. But even so, the memories I had of her were etched in my mind and not one of them was comforting.

"I don't think so," I said at last. "Our mother is ruthless and now I believe she is actually evil. I don't think either of us are like her." I shrugged, even though I was hurting inside. "I think she'd walk past us if we were lying sick on the ground."

"I've been called ruthless," said Arabella. She seemed to droop as she spoke. "I hope I'm not evil."

I patted her arm. "You're not evil," I said. "I think your parents used you badly and you grew up surrounded with their guilt and remorse. It's hardly surprising you wanted to get away from here."

Arabella let out a long breath. "This house has never felt like a home to me. Perhaps it would have been different if I had been a boy. My mother needn't have had much to do with me, and my father might have felt he'd made a better bargain."

"At least we both know the truth," I said. "You can call me an innocent, but I believe that this will change both our lives for the better." I felt my throat tighten. "At least, I hope it will."

"I don't want to die any more," said Arabella in a quiet voice. I did not dare ask about the baby. She squeezed my hand and an odd smile flickered over her face. "I must have repelled her," she said, as if she was talking to herself.

"Do you mean Aunt Frances?" I asked.

Arabella nodded. "Every time she looked at me, I must have reminded her of the she-devil they brought into their lives." She looked sideways at me. "I hope you don't mind."

"That's what Aunt Frances called her, too."

Arabella looked down at her hands. "Yet my father still lies. He still hopes that no one will find out what they did." Arabella shook her head. "I've seen him watching me since she died. He doesn't care about me. All he wants is to know for sure that she didn't tell me. Even though he knows she must have said something before she died." She covered her face with her hands and tears dribbled through her fingers. "I think I despise him as much as you do."

"He's your father," I said gently. "It will go easier if you can find a way to forgive him." As I spoke, I remembered pleading with Aunt Frances to tell Arabella the truth so she could forgive her.

It hadn't made any difference.

Arabella fell back against the pillows. The colour that had come back to her face was gone, and there were hollows around her eyes. "I don't understand why they want you to marry Suckley," she said, in a voice that was barely there.

I smoothed back her hair. "Don't think about that now. You need to sleep."

Arabella took my hand in her cold fingers and held it tightly. "I'm glad I have a sister."

"So am I."

We sat in silence for a couple of minutes. I found myself tracing a pattern of flowers woven into a Turkey carpet hung on the wall. When I turned back, Arabella was asleep.

I looked at her face to see if I could find anything of my mother's hard features. But there was nothing. I felt sure that Arabella must look like her paternal grandmother, just as I looked like mine.

She stirred in her sleep. I picked up a sheepskin from a chair and put it over her. She snuggled into the soft wool as if she was a child.

As I watched her, my heart swelled in my chest, but I wasn't quite sure why. It wasn't love or pity or even sadness. We were sisters. In less than a month, we would meet our mother together – me for the first time in seven years, Arabella almost for the first time in her life. It was not a moment I was looking forward to.

Part Two

BLEATHWOOD

Chapter Eleven

"Silence, my masters! *Silence!*"

The usher bellowed over the crowd that filled the Great Hall of Bleathwood. He was dressed in the black and green livery of Henry of Orgon and wore a felt hat with a feather. As he shouted he clapped his hands, as if he was moving through a throng of geese.

I had never seen so many people in one room. Men and women dressed as servants, in grey frieze with linen aprons, stood in groups talking with stewards and their ladies, wearing fine gowns and embroidered caps. Some of them held scrolls in their hands and looked serious. Others played games of dice on the floor and swapped apples and pieces of cake.

So far, no one had noticed me, which was exactly what I wanted. I needed to get a better sense of where I was before the long walk, which would end with a deep curtsey in front of the woman who called herself my mother.

From the moment I had seen the towers of the house standing up across the valley, and the dazzling pillars of light as the huge windows caught the afternoon sun, I understood. Bleathwood was all about showing off power and money on a scale that was a thousand times grander than my mother had known at Croft Amber. As we had drawn nearer and the cart had trundled along the road past well-tended fields and cottages, I remembered how ruthlessly my mother had run that estate. Here, she would hold sway over many more lives; and from what I understood from Arabella, Henry of Orgon was a quiet, scholarly man who by all accounts allowed her a free rein to do as she wished.

It reminded me of how she had lived with my father. I remembered Sam saying that there was no evidence of treason against Henry of Orgon, but I hadn't known then that it had been my mother who had wanted the Queen to visit Bleathwood. According to Arabella, she had been preparing for the visit for more than two years.

The work that had been carried out for the visit to Bleathwood was extraordinary. Fine new gardens had been laid out in front of the house with whitethorn and sweetbriar hedges planted neatly in star patterns, each one with a clipped yew bush at its centre. It was all surrounded by avenues of lime trees. There were fountains everywhere. The one in front of the house was particularly fantastic – a monstrous sea creature made of marble, spewing water from its jaws into a pool decorated with mermaids carved out of stone.

The rooms inside the house were just as elaborate. The plasterwork ceilings were so intricately moulded that they might have been made out of sugar. Walls were painted red and turquoise and yellow, and emblems and coats of arms were picked out in the glossiest gold and the shiniest black. Everywhere richly embroidered tapestries hung alongside Turkey carpets woven from silk.

But most incredible were the huge windows on every floor of the house. The glass on its own would have cost a fortune by any counting. Later, I found out that it was my mother who had insisted on the windows and that in the winter the house was colder inside than out. But what mattered to her was that she could look out from any window in the house and see her own land stretching away as far as the eye could see.

"Silence, my masters! Make way for Emerald St John." The usher of the house bellowed and clapped his hands. "Make way! Make way!"

I waited for him to call out who I was: "Make way for the daughter of Lady Millicent of Orgon," but there was nothing. That was when I realised that no one had acknowledged me as my mother's daughter since I had arrived in the house.

Emerald St John could be anyone. Yet I was here at her bidding to marry a man she had chosen against my will, after having ignored me for seven years.

Was this refusal to greet me as her daughter supposed to show her power over me right up to the end?

I felt sick at the thought of even looking at her face.

"Hold your nerve, sister," whispered Arabella's voice in my ear. "Her ladyship plays a game with you. Greet her as 'Mother' and this round will be yours."

"Arabella!" I cried. I had been looking for her since we arrived. Uncle Charles had refused to let us travel together, so I sat with Sarah in a covered wagon, and Arabella had been put in a stuffy coach with Hetty. Ever since the day he had shouted at me, I knew my uncle was suspicious of what we both knew and I can only think he didn't want to give us a chance to confide in each other during the long journey.

I turned the moment I heard Arabella's voice, but she was already standing in front of the usher, speaking rapidly and prodding him with her fan. I saw her point in my direction and his eyes widened with amazement as she spoke to him. It was enough to make the two women on either side of him turn round and stare at me.

"Silence, my masters! Make way for Emerald St John."

I kept my eyes on the floor as I walked down the hall and watched the white satin toes of my shoes appear and disappear under the hem of my gown. It was a beautiful dress made of yellow taffeta edged with embroidered rosebuds, each sewn with a seed pearl to look like a drop of dew. Sam had been as good as his word. The clothes that had arrived from Walsingham's office in London were gorgeous.

I thought of what Sarah had said as she fixed a lace cap to my hair: *I'd say your mother's face will pass for a plucked chicken's arse when she sees you, miss. Pretty as a garden, you are.*

I could feel my mother's eyes boring into me as I made

my way down the hall. They were light brown, flecked with gold, and had the crazy look of a goat. Even as a child I'd hated her eyes on me. Now, as I drew closer, I felt my stomach churning. So I did what I do when I go fishing. I took my thoughts to a secret place. This time I chose the vegetable garden at Hawkstone. It was a sunny morning and I was pruning a pear tree with the stubby-handled knife Aunt Frances had given me for my tenth birthday.

"Emerald St John!" The usher moved to one side in front of me and I swept a deep curtsey. Even in the hot, crowded room, the scent of jasmine and oak moss covered me like a cloud of steam. It was the heady perfume my mother had worn all her life; I'd forgotten what it smelled like, but now it all came rushing back. I rose from the curtsey and looked into the face I hadn't seen for seven years. Her cheekbones were sharper, but the coldness in her eyes hadn't changed.

"Mother," I said, in a firm, clear voice, "I am glad to see you."

My mother's face froze and the world stopped. I heard a bumblebee buzzing on the sunny window behind her. Whispers spread down the hall like ripples on a pond.

Arabella had been right. Some kind of game was being played, and from the look of her, it was plain that my mother hadn't expected to lose the first round.

She recovered quickly and stood to her full height, letting her eyes sweep over the hall like lantern lights. "Good men and women," she said in her deep, piercing

voice. "This is my daughter, who is welcome in our house."
She put out her arms and pulled me towards her with the
strength of a man. "You are more beautiful than I had
imagined," she whispered. Then, with a smooth movement that would have looked like a kind, light touch to the
assembled crowd, she turned me round and shoved me
back into the hall.

It was a miracle I didn't stumble. My head felt hot and
my clothes that had felt so fine and cool only moments
before now felt tight and damp with sweat.

I looked for Arabella in the blur of faces, but couldn't
see her. So I walked with my head held high, looking
straight in front of me. I had to get out into the air.
Otherwise I knew I would faint and my mother would be
able to pity me.

A man walked through the oak doors and stopped in
front of me. He had white hair and a kindly look on his
face. "Forgive me, madam," he said. "I am late to greet
you, but the welcome is no less for it. I am Henry of
Orgon. As the child of my esteemed wife, I hope that you
will feel very much at home here."

Arabella was right. He looked like a gentle, scholarly
man. If anything, he reminded me of my father.

Henry of Orgon led me out to the balcony and we
stood looking over the garden. As we exchanged courtesies, I realised with the strangest feeling that he knew
nothing about me and that he never once mentioned my
marriage to Suckley.

I suppose the confusion must have shown on my face.

"You look pale, mistress," said Henry of Orgon kindly. "Perhaps a rest after your journey?" He held up his hand and signalled to a servant to attend us. "This is a large house," he said, with the flicker of a smile. "I wouldn't want you to get lost."

I smiled in return and, as I followed the servant down a wide corridor hung with portraits and fine carpets, I asked myself for the first of many times during that visit, how such a gentle man had come to marry my mother.

Chapter Twelve

The attic room I shared with Sarah was hot and dusty, but it was empty, and that's all I cared about. I needed time to think.

I took off my gown and loosened my clothes. Someone had left a small jug of ale and a mug in the room and I realised I was very thirsty. I drank it all and sat down on the bed. I had expected my mother to announce my betrothal to Suckley when she greeted me. Indeed I had expected Suckley to be waiting for me beside her. But she'd said nothing and nor had anyone else. As for Suckley, there was no sign or mention of him. Not even a message from his manservant.

I rubbed my hands over my face. Part of me wanted to go and lie down, but the other part was getting more and more angry. How dare my mother and Suckley insult me like this?

"Miss, miss!" To my surprise, a little boy with a dirty, freckled face crept out from behind a chest in the corner of the room. His curly hair was black and matted and looked as if it had been chewed short by mice. As he came nearer the smell of bear grew stronger, and I saw it wasn't a boy at all.

"Meg!" I cried in amazement. "What are you doing here?"

Meg squatted by the side of the bed and held out a grubby hand like a puppy offering a paw. "I had to come, miss, truly I did. I'm your eyes and ears, miss, you said I was. I sneaked into Molly's cage, miss. Tom says he's going to sell me to the gypsies." She opened her eyes wide and went on in a pitiful voice, "You won't let him, miss. Promise me you won't."

I hugged her and breathed in the wonderful smell of bear. I'd never been so happy to see her.

"Bet you didn't know it was me," cried Meg gleefully. She pulled at her hair. "Did it myself with a kitchen knife and boot black."

Her face went serious. "The lordy lord's here, miss, an 'e's mad as a bee on a pin."

My heart skipped a beat. "Where did you see him?"

"I were in the stable loft," said Meg. "Tom's camped down by the duck pond and there's no spying to be done there so I hid with the 'orses. Anyway, in comes the maggoty ape telling everyone how important he is. And then this man pulls him off into a corner. Lucky for me, it were just below where I was. So he tells maggoty ape that no one in the house is to know his business or it'll be the worse for him. Her ladyship's orders."

171

Meg looked at me. "I swear he 'ad froth on his mouth, miss, 'e was so furious."

"What did he say?" I asked. It seemed impossible to believe that Suckley would listen to orders from a stranger.

"That were the odd bit, miss. The ape was frightened of him. Kept backing away like he 'ad a knife pointed at 'is gut."

"What did the man look like?"

"Nasty feller," replied Meg. "Head like a turnip and two slugs for a mouth." She looked at me. "It's right odd, miss, and Tom says so, too. Nobody in this place even knows who we are."

I made up my mind. I was going back downstairs. If Suckley was here, I wanted to see him for myself and find out what was going on.

"Help me straighten out this gown, Meg. Only don't get too close or we'll both stink of bear."

The door opened and Sarah walked in. She was carrying a bucket. "Tom said you'd be here." She sniffed and looked crossly at Meg. "What shall I do with her, miss?"

Meg turned to me with a piteous look on her face. "Please miss. Eyes 'n' ears, I am."

"Give her a wash and she can sleep with us," I said to Sarah.

Meg made a noise like a donkey and ducked under the bed as Sarah went to grab her.

I opened the door and stepped quickly into the corridor. The sooner I spoke to Suckley, the better.

* * *

172

When I came to the main staircase, I stopped and hid behind a marble statue of what might have been Hercules and listened to the voices. I wanted to pick out one; then I'd fit it to the face when I walked down the stairs.

A man began to speak and I felt as cold as the statue beside me. The voice wasn't coming from the hall below, it was coming from a door behind me.

"The man's a pig. Let him squeal. He'll do what he's told."

Another voice.

"We are agreed then."

The second voice was thin, with a mean, sneering note to it.

There was a groan of chairs moving over the floor and the sound of men getting to their feet. I stepped back to the top of the stairs and walked into the crowd to hide myself before the men came out from behind the door.

The first voice I'd heard had been deep with a French accent. I hadn't had to guess what the owner looked like. I already knew. It was Pierre Marchand and, as sure as a rock sinks in water, the pig he had been talking about was Suckley. Word must have got back that he'd been told to keep quiet and was furious.

A group of ladies stood around a long table covered with platters of sticky sweetmeats and dried fruits dipped in sugar. With their sparkling headdresses, they looked like beautiful birds gathered round a feeding tray.

I wrapped my shawl high round my neck and stood

173

beside a woman wearing a wide-brimmed red hat with a feather and a brown dress with full, black sleeves. She was tall, with broad shoulders. I sidled in behind her.

The door opened and the men came out of the room. There were three of them, dressed in silk doublets with stiff lace ruffs. They were laughing and whispering amongst themselves. Two of them were older men with full beards flecked with grey. The third man stood at the top of the stairs. Meg had described him perfectly. His head was turnip-shaped and his mouth looked like two slugs pressed together.

For all their easy laughter, the men moved self-consciously and their flat, snake eyes flicked back and forth over the room. They had no reason to bear me ill will, but I was glad of my neighbour's wide-brimmed red hat. I waited to see whether Pierre Marchand would join them, but there was no sign of him.

The men made their way across the crowded hall, calling out greetings as if they wanted to show that they knew everyone. Then they disappeared into the crowd.

I relaxed, and realised I was hungry. I went across to the table and picked up an almond paste biscuit flavoured with rose water. A servant stepped forward and poured me a cup of wine. Then I smelled rotten teeth and the mawkish stink of unwashed wool and I knew exactly who was behind me.

"I give you greetings, madam," said Lord Suckley. He stepped in front of me, blocking me against the table. "I was unaware of your arrival, else I would have sought you out sooner."

The ruff around his scrawny neck was as wide as a cart-wheel and made his face look like a shrunken apple on a stick. The lace cuffs at his wrists were already stained with food. He looked ridiculous.

"Lord Suckley." I dropped the smallest of curtseys and pretended not to notice his piggy eyes staring at my breasts.

He took my hand and raised it to his lips and I felt his warm spit trickle between my fingers.

"You flatter me with your beauty, madam," he said. "I am glad you are mindful of our agreement."

I overcame the urge to wipe my hand on the back of my gown, and began to play the part I had rehearsed as Sarah dressed me. "A small token of my esteem, Lord Suckley," I replied. I dropped my voice to an intimate whisper. "I swear, sir, I have never seen so many folk in so fabulous a place. I own I was rather nervous at it all."

I opened my fan and fluttered it prettily. "Oh my Lord," I cried. "I was so much the jelly, I didn't even know how I should address my mother! Would I say my lady, or dear madam?" I paused and let my eyes meet his. "Or should it be plain 'Mother'? After all, I haven't seen her for seven years."

I watched his face redden.

"Then my sweet Arabella whispered in my ear and at the last, I called her Mother," I said. "And it was the strangest thing, sir! I believe she was quite taken aback." I put a look of innocent puzzlement on my face. "Do you think she plays a game with us, sir? She doesn't speak of our marriage. And nor does anyone else. I shall ask Arabella. She's the only one who can make sense of things."

Suckley's face went from red to dark purple. "Don't take me for a fool, madam," he said furiously. "I have the contract with me. Our marriage will be settled. And I forbid you to seek Arabella's advice again. The woman is a fool and a troublemaker." He reached out, grabbed my arm and pinched it as hard as a horse bite.

I looked down at the marks his fingers had left on my skin and the part I had rehearsed left me. "I would rather play cards than continue this conversation with you," I said coldly. I snapped my fan in his face. "And I must tell you that I loathe cards." I made my way towards the carved marble fireplace to get as far from him as possible.

The woman in the red hat was standing with a younger woman on one side of the fire. She smiled at me and said, "Are you by any chance Emerald St John?"

"Yes, madam. I am pleased to make your acquaintance," I replied gratefully.

Her eyes reminded me of Aunt Frances and I warmed to her immediately.

"I am Evelyn of Lambeth," she said, "and this is my daughter, Lady Anne Bolton."

We curtsied and sat down together. Evelyn took a pack

176

of cards from a table. "We were about to play gleek and needed a third, so your company is well timed."

"Do you come to Bleathwood for the Queen's visit?" asked Lady Anne breathlessly. She was a small, round woman and reminded me of a pink and white sugar cake.

"We have journeyed from Sussex at Lord Henry's invitation," said Lady Anne. "Where are *you* from, madam?"

"Wales," I replied. "I travelled with my guardian, Sir Charles Mount." I widened my eyes to play the innocent. "Bleathwood is such a grand house. Even the upper chambers have windows!"

"Cold as ice blocks in the winter," remarked Evelyn of Lambeth drily. She picked up the cards and began to pull out the twos and threes of each house.

"Gleek is a child's occupation, mother-in-law," said a man's voice. It was thin and had a mean, sneering tone to it and I recognised it immediately. It was the man behind the door with the turnip head. "Why not play triumph? At least you need skill for that."

Evelyn of Lambeth stood up and said smoothly, "John, this is Emerald St John, Lady Millicent's daughter." She rested her hand on my shoulder and, to my astonishment, I felt the smallest pressure from her fingers.

I was a stranger to her. What could she be trying to tell me?

"Emerald, this is my son-in-law, Sir John Bolton."

"I am honoured, sir." I curtsied.

According to Meg, this was the man who had dragged

Suckley into a corner of the stables and told him to keep his mouth shut on my mother's orders. No wonder Suckley had been afraid of him. His eyes were as sharp as knives and he looked as vicious as a forest pig.

At that moment, Suckley strode over towards us and the hairs stood up on the back of my neck.

"I am confounded, madam," said John Bolton, ignoring the fact that Suckley was an arm's length away. "I had no notion you would be here. How fortunate for your mother."

I heard Suckley make a noise like a dog choking, but I managed to hold Bolton's gaze.

Lady Anne looked around in confusion. It was clear she thought something was wrong, but she had no idea what it was. Meanwhile, Suckley had moved too near not to be introduced.

"My dear sir." Lady Anne held out a plump arm towards him. "Forgive our poor manners." She introduced herself and her mother, smiling prettily, her teeth like pearls in her round, open face. "I fear I have not had the pleasure—"

"Suckley," came the furious reply. "At your service, madam."

John Bolton did not take his eyes off my face, and I could feel Evelyn Lambeth watching me, too. What had she meant by the squeeze of her fingers?

"Have you come far, Lord Suckley?" asked Lady Anne breathlessly, the only one behaving normally amongst us.

"Macclesfield," Suckley said shortly.

Lady Anne threw her gloved hands in the air. "Why, that is three days from here and the roads are little more than tracks in the mud!" She tipped her head to one side. "Are you one of Lord Henry's circle?"

Suckley squirmed like a sack of eels. He looked crushed and maddened and I realised he was near to losing control. I had to stop him from making even more of a scene.

"Lord Suckley and I met at my guardian's house in Wales last April," I said, making myself speak shyly but coolly. "We discovered that we would see each other again at Bleathwood for the Queen's visit." I turned to Lady Anne and matched her baby smile with my girlish one. "It is so exciting! I've never even seen Her Majesty, but I have a friend at Court and she tells me stories sometimes."

I gathered my skirts and curtsied again to Evelyn of Lambeth. "My thanks for your kind conversation, madam. Perhaps we shall play another time."

"I hope so." Her eyes met mine for a moment too long. I was sure now that this woman knew all about me yet I had no idea who she was at all.

"Why leave now, madam?" asked John Bolton, as if nothing untoward had taken place. "Surely you don't fear for your luck?"

"Not at all, Sir John." I turned to look steadily into Suckley's bulging eyes. "I feel most fortunate this evening. But it is late and I have travelled far."

Suckley moved beside me as if he couldn't stop himself.

"I would speak with you, madam," he said in a choked voice. "There are things these people should know."

My heart hammered in my chest and I felt John Bolton stiffen. What would he do if Suckley spoke out?

Bolton's pig eyes glittered nastily in his face. He cleared his throat and stood so near to Suckley, I half wondered if he had a knife point stuck into him.

"Emerald St John!"

A man wearing a black velvet cap and a green tunic appeared in front of me and bowed.

"I crave your indulgence, madam. The Lady Millicent begs you will attend her in her private chamber."

Chapter Thirteen

It was like walking into the belly of a whale. The room was entirely red. Swathes of burgundy damask hung from the walls, and the floor was stamped with a pattern of interlocking red circles. A dragon with red flames spewing from its mouth was painted on the ceiling, and its claws and long, scaly tail crept into every corner of the room.

At the far end, a lacquered chair sat between two candelabras, their candles filling the room with a smell of hot wax and cinnamon. On either side of the chair, red velvet floor cushions were piled against the wall.

I stood in the doorway, waiting for my mother to order me into her presence.

A voice said, "When did you last make sugar plate?" And Arabella stepped out of the shadows behind the chair.

"God's teeth, Arabella!" I said. There'd been enough surprises that night. "Sugar plate? Have you lost your wits? Why should I care about making candied decorations?"

Arabella stepped towards me and kissed me on both cheeks. "Why indeed?" she said as she led me to the cushions at the end of the room. "It was a skill I never learned. I was more interested in card tricks."

"Stop yacking like a mad woman," I said. "There are things we must talk about. I need your help."

"All in good time," said Arabella. "Now listen to me. The pastry cook rather inconsiderately sliced off his thumb while sculpting a unicorn for the Queen's table. Can you finish the job tomorrow morning?"

"Why can't our mother ask me herself?"

Arabella laughed. "She doesn't want her lack of kitchen skills broadcast through the house."

As she spoke, Arabella walked about the room, dragging her hands over the folds of damask as if she was feeling the wooden panels behind them. The shutters had been fastened and the room was dark except for the candle flame and the light that came through the edges of the windows.

"Hetty tells me you sleep on the third floor," said Arabella in a bemused voice. "She and I are in a cramped space with a dozen others."

She pulled back a large cushion that was propped against the end of a sideboard and peered behind it. "For my part, I am content. I am used to sleeping with company."

I watched as she lifted a carpet that was draped over a table and bent down to look underneath. I thought of Meg crouching under a table just like this one. Suddenly I understood what Arabella was doing, and why she was talking nonsense.

182

We came at last to the shutters at the end of the room.

"Will you open them?" I asked.

Arabella nodded.

A moment later, we stood side by side, looking out over the garden in front of the house.

Rows of glowing braziers had been arranged between the yew trees. In their light, the cones and balls of the clipped bushes were sharp and unnatural. Beyond the garden and the near pasture there were at least a dozen bonfires and I could see the dark outlines of tents and shelters and figures moving about.

The Queen's party was getting closer.

Arabella closed the shutters.

"No one spies on us," she said and poured out two cups of thin beer from a jug on the sideboard. "We have some time."

"It was our mother who summoned me."

"*Our mother* is giving a private banquet for her closest friends." Arabella swallowed a mouthful from her cup. "It was the master cook who summoned you, sister, because I struck a deal with him. In return for promising to make the sugar decorations for the Queen's table, we get a chance to speak on our own.

"Don't glare at me like that." Arabella laughed. "I've no intention of honouring my promise either." Her voice changed. "I need to speak with you."

"And I you, sister," I said. "No one in this house has heard of Suckley's name let alone any talk of my marriage

183

to him. He's been gagged on our mother's orders by a thug called John Bolton and he's as mad as a bull."

"I saw it all from the gallery," said Arabella. "It was sheer luck the master cook came past so I could get you away." She paused. "Who is the woman in the hat?"

"Evelyn of Lambeth. The baby-faced lady is her daughter, Anne. She's married to the thug Bolton."

"Whoever he is, Suckley's terrified of him," said Arabella.

"That's what Meg says. But why would he be so afraid of him?"

"It must be something to do with your mother."

"*Our* mother," I said.

"All right. *Our* mother." Arabella blew through her nose. "And that Lambeth knows more than she's letting on."

I remembered the squeeze of her fingers as she introduced me to John Bolton and the long look she had given me as I left. "I think she's trying to warn me of something."

"Did Suckley mention your marriage?" asked Arabella.

"He said he had the contract with him. Then your master cook saved me from him announcing it to the company."

"Did he say anything about me?"

It was an odd question. Why would Arabella care what Suckley thought of her?

"I told him we had no secrets from each other and he said you were a fool and a troublemaker and forbade me to speak to you."

A smile flickered over Arabella's lips. "No secrets," she said. "The ape's wrong on the other counts. The trouble's made and done and I'm no longer a fool."

Arabella finished her beer. "I've spoken to my father."

"About the child?" I blurted.

"Of course not, you idiot," said Arabella. "I told him I knew who my real mother was."

"*What?*" I couldn't believe my ears. "I thought we'd agreed to keep that secret!"

"The secret is that it was you who sat up all night with his dying wife and you who told me the truth. I didn't have to tell him that. He's lied to me all my life. I told him enough to make him uneasy. He'll be more manageable that way."

"What do you mean, 'manageable'?"

Arabella spread her fingers and took a deep breath and I sensed that I was about to hear the real reason why she wanted to speak to me.

"There isn't a lot of time left for me to save myself," said Arabella in a matter-of-fact voice. "Perhaps the Queen will take me back and perhaps there'll be a woman who will take the baby when it comes."

"So you'd have it?"

Arabella shrugged. "If I can't get rid of it. But I can't keep it if I don't have a husband." Her eyes went dull. "I wasn't smart enough to do a deal like our mother."

"Stop it, sister," I said gently. "You've hurt yourself enough already."

185

"Maybe I have and maybe I haven't," said Arabella. "At any rate, I've very little choice. If I can get a husband that will take me, I don't want any objections from my father." She shrugged. "And now he'll keep his mouth shut or the world will know what he did."

"That's madness, sister," I said. "You'd lose everything, too."

"I'll lose everything anyway if I don't do this."

She reached into the folds of her dress and took out a letter. "Read it. It's from Richard."

I stared at the letter and felt my head go cold.

Sam was dead!

That was why Arabella had gone to such trouble to talk to me on my own. I couldn't breathe and I felt my legs crumpling under me. I began to fall.

"God's death," cried Arabella. "Don't faint on me." She pulled me over to my mother's chair and sat me down. "Silly girl. Your lover is not dead if that's what you're thinking." She touched the tears on my cheeks and shook her head. "You must learn to hide what you feel."

I wiped away the tears with the back of my hand. "What does the letter say?"

"They're in Portsmouth."

"What? Oh my God!" My hands flew to my face and I began to cry all over again, this time with relief.

Arabella looked at me. "You really love him, don't you?"

"With all of my heart."

186

I took a handkerchief from my sleeve and cleaned up my face. "What will you say to Richard?"

"I don't know yet," replied Arabella. "Perhaps I'll have to tell him the truth."

"He'll never find out from me."

"Thank you."

There were shouts beyond the window and the sound of fireworks exploding.

We both started and jumped to our feet. My mother's private banquet must be over.

"She must not see us together," said Arabella. "I'm going back to the hall." She kicked the cushions into shape and I put the cups back on the sideboard.

There was muffled laughter on the landing, and the stamping of clogs on the stairs. When the voices faded, Arabella opened the door and looked quickly both ways. "Go," she said.

I kissed her quickly and ran across the landing and up the stairs.

As I turned the corner, I heard Arabella say, "You!"

"Well met," came the sarcastic reply. It was Suckley. "I would speak with you, madam."

I peeped round the corner. He had her by the wrist, and was pulling her.

"Let go of me!" cried Arabella furiously.

"That's not what you said last time I touched you," snarled Suckley.

"You are a lecher and, worse, you are a liar, sir," said

Arabella icily. "You gave me your word and I was idiot enough to believe it. You disgust me."

"Your opinion means nothing to me, harlot," sneered Suckley. "What weasel words did you have with John Bolton? What lies have you told him?"

I froze on the corner step, not daring to breathe. One sound would give me away.

"John Bolton and his papist cronies are no friends of mine," snapped Arabella. She yanked back her arm. "They are villains, sir – only you are too fool to see it."

There was a clatter of footsteps as Arabella fled, then silence.

I heard Suckley spit. "Bawd," he muttered under his breath. "You'll have the pox to thank me for, soon enough."

Chapter Fourteen

Meg was curled up on a straw pallet when I opened the door to our chamber, but she jumped up as soon as she heard me.

"Lordy lord couldn't get a place in the house," she said. "'E's had to take lodgings at The Lamb on the Oxford Road."

"Are you sure?"

"Sure as a wart on a witch's chin, miss," replied Meg. She sidled up to me and fixed me with beady eyes. "An' Hetty says Miss Arabella's for leavin'."

I stared at her. "How does she know?"

"It's the only reason, Hetty says. Why else won't she unpack her lovely new clothes?"

I knew the reason, but I was glad that Hetty hadn't guessed. They were too small to fit round her middle.

I lay back against my pillows and blew out my candle. Every part of my body felt like lead, but all I could think of was Sam leaning forward on his mare and galloping towards me. I held his locket in my fingers and prayed that he would arrive safely. Then I closed my eyes and fell instantly asleep.

I dreamed I was standing in a cold, slimy cellar in front of a slate table. I was rolling out sugar plate and everything I touched was sticky because my fingers were covered with sugar and starch and gum.

The floor was covered in the yolks and shells of the eggs I had cracked. You need lots of egg white to make sugar plate and every time I moved, my feet slithered in goo and broken shell.

My mother sat on a high stool under a small barred opening, high in the wall. She wore a purple cape lined with wolf fur and her long fingers were covered in sharp, sparkling rings. Every time I finished a piece of sugar plate, she took a new mould down from a shelf and put it beside me. She didn't tell me what to do. I did it without speaking, as if I was a trained slave.

I took the mould in my hand and dusted it with sugar and gold leaf. Then I pressed the paste into the corners and set it down to dry. Hundreds and hundreds of moulds were waiting to be emptied and they were all kinds of sizes and curious shapes and figures.

As I bent over the table my back ached, and I felt as if I had worked in that damp, whitewashed room all my life. So many decorations had to be made for the Queen's table and each one of them had to be perfect.

I'd already made the bear pit. The curved moulds for

the walls had dried quickly. When I had brushed off the loose sugar with a hare's tail, I'd painted them in the Queen's favourite colours which were scarlet and gold, each one with her own crest on the top.

My fingers ached as I held the fine brushes and painted each tiny figure without a smear before fitting them in their place.

The Queen sat in the middle on a carved throne looking down over rows of seats to the centre of the pit. Her spun-sugar dress was orange and yellow and her eyes were two chips of white icing. Figures of important ladies and gentlemen in bright clothes sat on either side of her and my mother stood behind her. I had painted her in red with a gold chain set with jewels around her neck. There was a place for Henry of Orgon, but his figure wasn't finished yet.

Even though I was in the cellar, I could hear the noise of the crowd like a hive of bees trapped in my head. It seemed impossible that my mother couldn't hear it, too, but she only handed me the moulds and said nothing.

I painted the last figures and put them down in the middle of the pit. It was a man with two black dogs on the end of a rope. The dogs stood on their hind legs and were almost as tall as the man. Their teeth were bared, and painted pink and white to show froth on their jaws.

My mother stepped down from her stool. I could see she was holding a figure in her fingers, but I couldn't meet her eyes. I watched her put the figure on the ground in front of the dogs. At first I couldn't make out what it was. The round, brown shape that was the sugar body had collapsed in the middle and was painted red. I looked more closely. It was a bear lying on its back, its legs hanging floppy like a broken toy. Where its stomach should have been was a ragged, red hole.

My mother stood back to admire her work. "I made this from a drawing I did." She reached out her hand and lifted up my chin so I had to look at her. "After I met you."

Her eyes turned into balls of fire and I woke up shrieking.

My shift and nightcap were soaked in sweat. I heard a strange noise halfway between a sob and a wail, and realised it was coming from me.

I made myself lie still to stop the screaming in my head. I saw the bucket in the corner and the empty pallet on the floor. It was then that I heard the noise outside the window.

I jumped up and looked out.

It was as if a small town was advancing on Bleathwood; but it was a town of carts and carriages and wagons. One cart caught my attention. It had the royal coat of arms painted on the side and it was stacked with furniture roughly tied down under sheets of canvas. Even from my window, I could make out four pillars as thick as trees joined to a carved, rectangular frame.

I was looking at the Queen of England's bed.

There was a knock at the door. "Emerald? Are you there?"

I recognised the voice immediately, even though my Uncle Charles was the last person I had expected at this time in the morning. I wrapped a shawl round my shoulders and opened the door.

He was standing in the hallway and I knew straight away that something was wrong. His face was hollow, his skin as grey as a wood-wasp's nest. He opened his mouth to speak, but I shook my head. Anyone could be listening to us.

I said, "Come in and sit down."

Normally I would have made apologies for the unmade bed and the tangle of clothes and last night's water still in the bucket; but I said nothing. The time for courtesies was over.

He sat down on a stool by the fire beside the pallet where Sarah and Meg had been sleeping, and for a moment neither of us spoke. His shoulders were slumped and bony, and I noticed his hair had become thin over his scalp.

"Arabella didn't sleep in her bed last night," he said, head in his hands. "Hetty believes she's gone to London." He looked up at me and his eyes were thick with misery. "Emerald, I have lied to you and used you badly."

"Uncle—" I began.

"No." He rubbed his hands over his face. "I came here to ask about Arabella. But for another reason, too. Please, let me speak what is on my mind. It will be the last thing I ever ask of you."

I didn't know what to say, but he didn't seem to notice.

He said, "Ever since Frances died I have prayed for God's guidance, but He has given me none. Perhaps it is what I deserve."

He took a deep breath. "I know it was you who sat up with Frances when she died. She would have called for you, not Arabella, and you would have gone to her."

I couldn't reply. It was the first time I'd heard the truth. Arabella had lied to him and he had known it.

At the sound of his voice, I understood that none of the hurt and sadness I had inside me had gone away, and it was all I could do not to cry in front of him.

"I was wrong not to question Arabella when I came back to Hawkstone that night," said my uncle, in a voice I could barely hear. "But I couldn't bear to accuse her of lying to me about the death of the woman she had known as her mother."

He took a deep breath, as if what he had to say hurt like a burn. "Frances loved you, and she needed to be forgiven before she died."

His shoulders trembled. "She loved me once, but she never forgave herself for what we did. We both wanted to have a child, but she accepted God's will, and I couldn't."

He turned away, as if he couldn't bear to look at me. "I persuaded Frances to pass off Arabella as her own and she despised me for it."

The room was still, and so full of misery I thought I would choke on it. Once I'd believed I would hate this man for ever for what he had done. Now I knew I couldn't. It wasn't right to let anyone suffer like this.

I said, "I begged Aunt Frances to tell Arabella, but she refused to." I spoke as gently as I could.

"Frances loathed Arabella from the moment she saw her," said my uncle, as if he was talking to himself. He put his face in his hands again. "My poor, sweet daughter! She never knew a mother's love and she was innocent. I will be damned for what I did."

I took his hand. I wanted to say something to him that would make him suffer less, so I told him that Arabella and I were glad to be sisters and that there was a bond between us now that could never be broken. But I couldn't tell him that Arabella was carrying Suckley's child and that was why she had gone. The child was her secret and I would never betray her.

As for Suckley, I had no idea what part he had played in my mother's game, but I prayed that by keeping my mouth shut, I was playing out a rope with which he would hang himself and the people around him.

My uncle put his hand on mine and I was glad to feel its warmth. "There is evil in this house," he said, "and we are all caught up in it. I fear for you and Arabella."

"Nothing makes sense to me," I replied. "Nobody mentions my marriage, and my mother barely acknowledges me. Suckley has fury in his face, but is forced to say nothing."

My uncle groaned. "If only I had sent back Millicent's letter."

"What do you mean?"

"I had a chance to object to your marriage," replied my uncle miserably. "I had a chance to call her bluff, but I was too frightened she would expose Arabella. Frances was disgusted with me."

"It wouldn't have made any difference," I said, as kindly as I could manage. "Suckley is part of some plan and so am I."

It occurred to me that my uncle might have an idea why my mother would get involved with a man like John Bolton. She was no Catholic, even if her husband was. I remembered Sam had told me how some men believe in their right to kill a tyrant. If anyone looked like a killer, it was Bolton. Henry of Orgon's face floated into my mind again. Was he really a kindly scholar, or was there a traitor behind those gentle looks?

"What do you know of Henry of Orgon?" I asked carefully.

Uncle Charles looked at me. "I've never met him before," he said. He paused. "I don't want to upset you, but I want you to know what I think."

"You may speak honestly," I said.

"It seems to me that he is very like your father." My uncle shook his head. "In fact, I can't imagine how he could have agreed to marry the woman who is your mother."

I didn't take my eyes from his. I knew it was a difficult thing for him to say. "I'm grateful for your honesty," I said. "The same thought had gone through my mind." I took a breath and said the thing which had been haunting me. "Aunt Frances called her a she-devil. It's as if she has a witch's power over a man."

The colour drained from my uncle's face and his eyes filled with anguish and guilt.

"She has," he muttered.

I said nothing. The thought was too unbearable.

Outside the window, someone began to beat a drum and there was the sound of bells ringing.

My uncle stood up and ran his hands over his drab, grey doublet. I knew he wanted to say something before he left me. But he looked so sad, I took his hand in mine. "If I hear any news of Arabella, I promise I will tell you."

He leaned forward and kissed my forehead. Then the door closed behind him.

It was odd but after my uncle left my head felt clear for the first time in a long while. I suddenly saw things as they truly were. I understood now the depth of my love for Sam and the fearsome evil of my mother's nature and I began to wonder for the first time whether there was a madness in her.

The dreadful dream I'd had fluttered in my mind and I knew I had to go to Molly straight away. As I pulled on the breeches and jacket that Sarah had hidden for me in a sack at the bottom of the chest, I thought of my mother's second letter and her determination to bring Molly to Bleathwood. It was all about ruthlessness and cruelty.

She was obsessed with both, and Molly was a symbol of her power over me. It was true that the Queen was entertained by the sight of her dogs mauling a helpless bear, but the real truth was that my mother wanted to show the world that she could use me and anything I cared for as she wished.

When I was a child, I'd read about a ferocious female spider who ate her mate and anything that strayed too near her. That was what my mother felt like to me.

For some reason, I wasn't frightened for Arabella. Wherever she was or whatever she had decided to do, I believed that she wasn't in danger and that she would be able to look after herself, just as I intended to do.

We were sisters, after all.

I looked at my face in the mirror, stuffed my hand into the chimney, rubbed soot round my eyes and blackened a front tooth. Then I pulled up my hair and pushed it under a cloth cap. When I had finished, I looked enough like a servant lad to get away with it if I kept my head down.

Chapter Fifteen

"'Strewth, miss, I didn't know it was you!" Sarah dropped the petticoat she was carrying and helped me to my feet. "You were running so fast, I couldn't move out the way." She straightened her apron. "Beggin' your pardon, miss, but you're wanted."

My heart sank. In another minute, I would have been through the back door and into the yard where no one would have noticed a lad with a dirty face.

"Who wants me?"

Sarah picked up the petticoat and shook it out. "Master cook's boy has been up to me twice. Swears you and Miss Arabella promised to be in the kitchen this morning." She scowled. "I told him to stuff hay in his gob. What would you be doing in the kitchen, miss?"

"Making sugar plate," I said. I saw the painted figures in my nightmare, and shuddered. "Not any more, though. My mother can do her own fancy work."

"What's happened to you, miss?" asked Sarah. "When I

left this morning, you were asleep like a baby. Now every-thing's topsy-turvy again. I can feel it."

"Arabella's gone missing," I said. "Hetty's giving out she's run away and Sir Charles is half mad with worry."

"I'm glad to hear it," said Sarah. "Some father he's been."

I drew her aside to let a girl carrying a bucket twice her size stumble past us.

"Everything is different, Sarah," I said in a low voice. "He has asked me to forgive him."

"Why should you?" demanded Sarah. "It's not my place, miss, but that man handed you over like a trussed bird just so he could save his own skin. He'll be damned for what he did."

"He knows that." I paused. "It's my mother who is truly bad, Sarah."

Sarah's face reddened. She'd always had the gift to see people's real nature as if there was a coloured light above their heads. "I know that, miss," she said. "I saw it straight away." She shuddered. "Your mother's got the devil's black marks all over her."

"And Arabella?" I asked suddenly. "Does she have the same marks?"

Sarah looked down at her hands. "I'd like to say differ-ent, but no, she hasn't."

A boy in servants' livery stamped up the stairs towards us. Last night he had served me wine. I turned my face to the wall so he didn't recognise me.

"A message for Emerald St John," he said to Sarah. He looked at me and held his nose. "*Phwoah*! What's that stink?"

"Bear," replied Sarah in a matter-of-fact voice. "Who sent you?"

"His Lordship, Henry of Orgon." The boy reached inside his tunic and took out a small box and a piece of folded parchment sealed with wax. "I'm to give this to her. No one else."

"Don't be foolish, boy," said Sarah. "You know who I am or you wouldn't have stopped me." She held out her hand.

"Can't," said the boy pulling back the box. "It's her or no one. I'll get a beating otherwise."

"Give it to me and save yourself a beating." I took off my cap, and my hair fell on my shoulders. "You know who I am. You served me wine last night."

The boy's mouth dropped open and his eyes bulged like a startled rabbit. I took the box and the letter from his hand. "This is my costume for the Queen's entertainment tomorrow."

"No need to spoil your master's surprise," said Sarah. She squeezed the boy's ear between her thumb and finger. "Do you understand me?"

"Yes, miss! I swear, miss!" He turned and fell over his feet to get away.

I broke the seal and unfolded the letter. "I'm invited this evening to bid the Queen welcome." I read on. "The gift is from my mother."

I handed the folded letter to Sarah and opened the box. Inside was a black velvet drawstring pouch. Inside the pouch was a dark red stone, set in silver and fixed with a pin to a piece of white fur. It looked like a drop of blood in my hand.

"It's an agate," said Sarah. "It's supposed to change your nature so you'll do her bidding. Bury it."

I shook my head. "I won't be frightened by her." The stone stayed cold in the heat of my hand.

Sarah looked at me curiously. "I'll have a hot bath waiting when you come back," she said.

I smiled. "Are you suggesting I smell of bear, Sarah?"

She smiled back. "It's not a suggestion, miss."

Bleathwood was ten times the size of Hawkstone. In the back courtyard there were two breweries and a bakehouse, as well as larders for game and fish and meat and storerooms for flour and sacks of dried beans.

Beyond the courtyard were the high brick walls of the vegetable garden and a patchwork of meadows and cornfields.

Meg had said Tom was camped by the duck pond. But for all I knew the duck pond was five meadows away. I stopped at a grassy triangle with three tracks in front of me. A laundry woman with forearms as thick and red as hams was laying out sheets on a hedgerow.

"What you doing there, boy?" she bellowed. "There's work for idlers."

"Cook sent me to fetch duck eggs," I shouted.

"Get on with it!" She waved towards the middle track. "You knows where to go." She straightened as she spoke and stared.

I felt hair on my face and shoved it quickly under my cap.

I was gone before she could take another look at me.

It was a narrow track with cracked puddles where the ground had dried out and a line of rough grass was growing down the middle. On either side carts and wagons were pulled up in the fields. Bonfires smouldered and horses were tethered to stakes in the ground, munching grass, nostrils snorting steam in the early morning chill.

The duck pond was the size of a small lake, surrounded by reeds. I could smell the bad egg stink of stagnant water before I saw it. I breathed it in and smiled to myself. After the smell of bear, I liked the smell of stagnant water because it reminded me of Hawkstone.

When I was a child, I used to sit on the edge of the duck pond at sunrise and watch the scummy water turn from dark grey to brilliant green as the pale light crept over the surface. It was a time to think and if you were very quiet, a time to watch the insects and animals wake up and move about.

I sat down on a flat rock to calm myself before I saw Molly for the first time. A frog croaked in the reeds beside me and I heard a *plop* as it jumped into the pond.

I picked up a stone and flipped it into the pond. The scum wobbled and a dark circle of water appeared. I imagined Sam rising like a curl of mist and coming to sit close beside me, his arm round my shoulder. A longing for him spread through me like heat from the sun.

The fire outside Tom's cart was still burning, but the wooden door of Molly's cage was open and the cage was empty. I climbed up the steps and put my head inside. The smell was choking, but the straw was clean and an old red wool blouse I'd given Tom to put in her cage for the journey was scrunched up in a corner.

Tom's voice hollered from the field. "Get ya away, else I'll chase ya!"

He was running across the meadow with Molly lumbering beside him. I jumped down from the cage and ran towards them, shouting Molly's name.

At the sound of my voice, Molly snorted and whinnied and Tom's shout turned into a greeting.

When I stopped in front of Tom, neither of us knew what to do. In the end I stuck out my hand like a boy and Tom took it in his. Which was just as well since Molly buried her snout in my stomach and gave me such a push I nearly fell over.

"Meg said you would be here," I said, tucking in the shirt that had come away from the breeches.

"That rapscallion!" said Tom. "I never believed it when she sneaked out of the straw. She was away before I could catch her!"

He bent down and rubbed Molly's head. "Mind you, it's on account of Meg that the bear's in good heart."

"It made me happy to see her," I replied. I paused. "This is a strange house, Tom."

"Load of tricky papists, if you ask me," muttered Tom. "I'll be glad when we're gone."

Molly growled at the back of her throat and rubbed her head against my leg.

"She looks well," I said. I patted the thick fur around her neck.

"More's the pity. There's no point in pretending," said Tom bluntly. "It's a bad place for people and animals alike. They say an old bear's bin brought in this morning with a pack of the Queen's mastiffs in the wagon behind him."

"They've built a bear pit and a banquet tent in front of the house." I held his eyes. "It's for the Queen's entertainment tomorrow and we have to make a plan for it."

Molly tilted her head as if she was listening.

"Maybe she won't be needed if they's got an old 'un," said Tom.

I shook my head. Now it was hard to stop my voice from trembling. "There are certain people who want to see the dogs on Molly. Whether or not there's an old bear before her."

205

There was silence, then Tom said, "We knew that from the beginnin', lass."

"Yes."

Tom reached into his pocket and fed Molly an apple. "She remembers her tricks well enough," he said, as if he was changing the subject. "I bin taking her through them with a sack of corn on her back."

He handed me Molly's rope. "Will you go through it with her once? It'll help her no end, and I can see you be dressed for it."

"That's why I'm here," I said. I made myself smile at him. "Wish me luck."

"Ain't nothing to do with luck, miss," said Tom. "You an' the bear understand each other. That's what matters."

I shortened the rope and set off across the meadow with Molly at my side. Men and women cutting hay stopped and watched us. I waved to them and pretended they were fine ladies and gentlemen and when my stomach filled with butterflies, I cursed myself for being faint-hearted.

I began to run faster. "Come on, Molly!" I cried. "Close now, and I'll jump!"

Her fur touched my leg as I fell in with her stride. Then, with a shout to warn her, I jumped on to her back, grabbed the thick rolls of skin around her neck to steady myself and held on with my knees. Once I was steady, I held up my arm and whooped with triumph.

When we came back to camp, I could see Tom was

pleased with us. "That were well done, miss," he said. He gave Molly some scraps and tied her to the door of her cage. "Now sit you down and we'll think what to do tomorrow."

Chapter Sixteen

I don't know why I picked so many wildflowers on my way back to the house. Perhaps I had a notion to brighten the room I shared with Sarah and Meg and remind us all of Hawkstone.

By the time I reached the back courtyard, I had a huge bunch of yellow daisies, cornflowers and poppies all wrapped round with a strand of ivy from the hedge.

A young woman dressed in the black-and-green colours of the house came up to me. She was holding half a dozen pigs' ears threaded on a string.

"Who's them flowers for?" she said in a friendly voice. She smiled. "Don't often see a stable boy pickin' flowers."

I blushed. I'd forgotten what I looked like.

Then it occurred to me that she might have heard some tittle-tattle. "What's the talk of your mistress's daughter that's marrying the lord?" I asked.

"Ain't heard no talk of that," replied the girl. She looked at me proudly. "An' I would 'ave because I was servin' at supper last night." She reached into her smock and handed me something brown and greasy. "Lord Henry's hedgehog, this is. It's got dates in it."

I put the food in my mouth, but I barely tasted it. If my mother's servants hadn't heard about a marriage then no marriage was ever planned in the first place. I held out my hand for another bit. This time I tasted cinnamon and pork meat. I sucked my fingers clean. "What's your name?"

The girl smiled at me. "They calls me Jane Three cos two sisters died before I came along." She jerked the pigs' ears in her hand. "I'm goin' to the bear pit. You comin'?"

I couldn't believe my luck. "If you's askin'," I said, trying to talk like a stable lad and setting off beside her. I pointed at the pigs' ears. "Them's for the dogs?"

"Ar." Jane Three dropped her voice. "There's a big old bear in a cage down there," she said. "Me and the pot scourer prodded 'im last night."

We turned down a pathway hidden between two hawthorn hedges that followed the shape of the formal gardens in front of the house. Through the leaves, I could see the coloured gravel glittering in the sunshine. There was the sound of splashing water and ladies' voices chattering. I stopped for a moment and peered through the hedge to see if I could catch a glimpse of Arabella, but she wasn't there.

At the far end of the garden, the ground sloped away to a river. Halfway down the slope stood a timber-framed banqueting hall painted gold and silver and decorated with the Queen's crests.

In front of the timber-framed hall was a round bear pit sunk into the ground and surrounded by rough wooden palings. Rows of narrow benches rose steeply on three sides.

Jane Three held her finger to her lips. We crept round the outside of the house and peered in through the window spaces. The single room was lined in turquoise velvet and the ceiling had been painted with hundreds of tiny stars arranged in constellations: the Great Bear and the Little Bear with the Hunter between them.

It was the stuff of dreams and I was so taken aback by it that I didn't notice Jane Three had gone and I was on my own. Then I heard hounds snarling and yapping. It was the noise dogs make when they fight over food. In my mind, I saw sharp teeth ripping apart the fleshy pink pigs' ears.

I had to go. The sound was making me want to scream.

I ran back up the path between the hedges. Then I heard voices coming round a corner a few feet in front of me and I stopped dead in my tracks.

"Fortunately met, dear madam!" It was a man speaking, high and piping, and I imagined a beardless face with full lips. "The sweet pleasures of this morning are gathered for you!"

"Your courtesy flatters me," replied a woman's voice. "But the sun's warmth is a heavenly gift."

I heard titters of laughter and the sound of a small dog yapping.

"Your servant, dear Majesty," replied the first voice. It was as if a game was over.

My legs turned into wet string. There was no place to hide and no time to run so I held out the flowers that were still in my hand and bowed so low my head almost touched the ground.

I heard a *crunch* of footsteps on the pathway.

A strong smell of marjoram filled the air and I saw a pair of patterned silk shoes beside another pair of leather boots with gold buckles on the ground in front of me. A second later, more shoes appeared. I didn't look up.

I knew people were standing in front of me and felt an edginess in the air as if no one knew what to say. On the one hand, the Queen guarded her privacy. On the other, it was known she liked surprises if they were amusing.

"Summer's child salutes Gloriana," piped the high voice nervously.

I'm sure it was the flowers that saved me.

There was silence. Then the Queen said, "Look up, boy."

Her face was the strangest thing I had ever seen. Her skin was like tree bark painted with limewash and there were patches of rouge on her cheeks. But even though her eyes were sunk into pockets of wrinkles, they were clear blue and looked into mine as if she could read every thought in my head.

I was so terrified that my mind went blank. "Welcome, your Queenliness," I said, and gave her my flowers.

Her pencil-thin lips shaped themselves into a smile.

"Methinks you stink of bear," she replied. A courtier took the flowers and she swept past me.

"*Your Queenliness?*" chortled Meg. "You daft flap-dragon, miss!" She pushed my wet bath sheets into a heap. "Her Mooniness could have chopped off yer 'ead then and there!"

"Enough of the flap-dragon, Meg," chided Sarah. "Mop up the floor and take those sheets out of here."

"What if Her Holiness sees you at supper?" demanded Meg. She held up her mop like a pitchfork and prodded the sheets with it. "What if she orders you to be taken to the Tower, miss?"

"Then you shall come with me, Meg," I said. "I expect I'll need a spy there, too."

"Off with you now," said Sarah firmly. "And take some meat scraps to Tom while you're out."

Meg pushed the sheets out of the door and came back for the parcel of meat scraps. "What's them things in your hair, so I can tell Tom?"

"Seed pearls and carnations," said Sarah, who had been dressing my hair for the last hour.

Meg opened the door. "And what colour would you call that dress you's wearing?"

"Azure," I said.

"Azure." Meg repeated the word as if it was a piece of sugar in her mouth. "You look like a queen, miss," she said. "Better than Her Wrinkliness any day."

* * *

212

I stood at the top of the grand staircase leading down to the Great Chamber and looked at the two portraits that hung on the wall. One was of Henry of Orgon sitting at a writing desk. He had a quill in one hand and an open book in front of him. There was a skull on the shelf behind him. It was a good likeness. His features were still and his eyes looked inwards as if he was absorbed in his own thoughts. The portrait of my mother showed a woman in fine clothes, looking through a window at meadows and forests. Her lips were parted and there was an expression of physical pleasure on her face. It was another good likeness.

I sensed someone watching me. John Bolton was standing behind me, picking his teeth with a twig.

My first thought was to ignore him, but then I changed my mind. I needed to know about Suckley.

"My compliments, sir," I said, dropping the smallest of curtseys. "Have you seen Lord Suckley? I was taken away unexpectedly last night and wish to speak with him."

"Lord Suckley is gone to London, madam," said Bolton.

"Are you quite sure, sir?"

"I sent him myself," he replied.

His piggy eyes shifted and I knew he was lying. He had no idea where Suckley was. But why would he lie to me?

I swept past him and walked down the steps.

The grand ornamental beds in front of the house had been transformed into a scene from the Arabian Nights. Lords and ladies dressed in flowing silks, some with veils covering their faces, wandered amongst pavilions made of satin and decorated with flowers and ivy.

I found myself walking towards a group of musicians playing by the fountain. The songs they sang were from the country. The sound of their fiddles and recorders reminded me of the village players at Hawkstone.

I took a path I hadn't seen before and wandered to the edge of the garden. The path turned away from the house and followed a line of poplars. At the end, I could see a meadow that was bright with buttercups. I felt an urge to stand in the middle of the yellow flowers in my azure dress, so I went down the path.

There was a cottage on the far side of the meadow. It was a pretty place, built of stone with white carved lintels and a weather vane in the shape of a unicorn in the middle of the pitched roof. Around the cottage was a garden planted with country flowers. From where I was standing I could see roses and hollyhocks and clumps of sweet-smelling gillyflowers. In the middle of the beds was a brick well, its shingle roof painted red.

There was something of a fairy tale about it all. It was the kind of place some great lady from London might come to for a sunny afternoon and pretend to be a country wife.

Two black-and-white spaniels ran out of the front door and began to snuffle round the garden, yapping at mice. I pulled back behind an oak tree and waited.

My mother appeared on the doorstep, with Pierre Marchand by her side.

My eyes felt as if they were glued open on my face. I was sure that Suckley would follow them out because they would have all been discussing my marriage arrangements. I waited and prayed that the little dogs were as silly as they looked and that they wouldn't smell me for the mice.

Suckley never appeared.

I watched as my mother held out a piece of paper and she and Marchand began talking in low voices. It took me a moment to realise they were both speaking French. I tried shutting my eyes and concentrating on their voices, but the dogs didn't stop yapping and I could hardly make out a word, so I watched their faces instead.

Marchand's face looked dark and angry. His hands jerked about in the air as he spoke. He wasn't at all the assured man I remembered from Hawkstone.

I saw my mother put her hand on his arm. It was a strangely intimate gesture for a woman of her standing to make to a perfumier. It made me think she was giving him strength, telling him to be patient, asking for his trust. Something about the pair of them was so disturbing that my stomach filled with spiders and I had to hold on to the tree trunk to keep myself steady.

The dogs stopped yapping.

"*Courage, Comte*," I heard my mother say, as if she was talking to a child. "It is all going well. You will have your prize and success will be ours tomorrow."

To my utter astonishment, she leaned forward and

kissed him on the cheek. Then he turned back through the door.

My eyes were aching, but I couldn't drag them away. My mother walked towards a clump of blue monkshood on the other side of the house. I couldn't see her face, but I didn't have to. I knew she was in a rage. As she passed the tall, blue flowers, she picked up a stick and knocked off all the petals with one vicious swipe.

Despite what she'd told the Frenchman, it was obvious everything was not going well at all.

I sat down by the fountain carved like a sea monster and looked into the pool of water. My head felt as if it was full of fish, too, all swimming in different directions.

It didn't surprise me that Pierre Marchand was not the perfumier he had pretended to be. None of his talk at Hawkstone had rung true. Everything about him was aristocratic and assuming. He was not in the service of a French count, he *was* the count. I remembered then that he had told me the name of the family he supposedly served. What was it? I raked over the conversation we'd had. Nothing came back to me; except that whoever they were, they came from Normandy.

But his name was not important. The point was, how was he involved with my mother? And why had he come with Suckley to see me at Hawthorne? It was clear that he had nothing but contempt for his travelling companion.

I let my mind go back to that visit. The Frenchman had

made a point of asking questions around the house. He had even gone down to the stables to look at Molly, which had seemed odd at the time. Now I was sure he had been following my mother's instructions.

But what had they been talking about outside the cottage? What was the prize my mother had promised the Frenchman? Surely they weren't planning to murder the Queen in front of hundreds of guests? Besides, there were special tasters at all of the banquets she attended. It was almost impossible to poison her food. Even so, I knew now that whatever they were planning would happen tomorrow.

I looked around at the ladies and their gentlemen talking in the warm sunshine amongst the clipped hedges and glittering gravel paths, hoping to see Arabella. She might be able to make sense of all this. But there was no sign of her.

Water pattered out of the fountain and I leaned back and let my mind fill with thoughts of Sam. I was sure I would be able to sense him if he was near, but all I felt was longing and, at the edges of my mind, the first prickling of fear. Apart from my uncle, there was no one I could trust to protect me from whatever fate my mother had planned for me.

At that moment, Evelyn of Lambeth walked past. She stopped beside me as if to look at the fish and spoke quietly from behind her fan. "Don't turn," she said. "People are watching us."

"Why should I trust you?" I asked, even though I did as I was told. "John Bolton is your son-in-law."

"I warned you of Bolton last night," replied Evelyn. "He is a dangerous man and I did not choose him to marry my daughter."

"He's in the service of my mother," I said. If she denied it, I'd walk away.

But she said, "That is true — and you, of all people, must be on your guard."

"Why are you telling me all of this?" I asked. "We don't know each other."

Evelyn paused for a moment. "You know my son," she said in a low voice. "Sam's father was my first husband."

I looked sideways at her face and suddenly saw the likeness. It was so strong I don't know why I hadn't seen it before.

I gripped the edge of the fountain to steady myself. "Did Sam ask you to look after me here?" I asked in a choked voice.

"I can't answer that," replied Evelyn. "It is enough for you to know who I am."

My head spun with questions. "What is going on in this house, Evelyn?" I asked. "I believed I was brought here to marry Suckley. But it's not true. My mother never intended the marriage to take place."

"Of course she didn't," said Evelyn. "She's testing her power over you."

"There's more to it than that." I told her what Meg had overheard in the stables. "So Suckley's been gagged, but he's here for a reason, I'm sure of it."

218

I watched the fish. Had Sam told his mother about the plot against the Queen? It was impossible to guess and I didn't want to give anything away. But now I knew I could trust her and I didn't feel so frightened that I was on my own. She might even be able to help me.

"Do you know of a man called Pierre Marchand?" I asked. "He came with Suckley to see me in Wales."

"What does he look like?"

I described Marchand quickly. "He has the face of a baby, no beard and the palest eyes you could ever imagine."

"That's Comte Landemer," she said. "He is nephew to Henry of Orgon."

In my mind, I heard the French voice on the other side of the door again. *The man's a pig. Let him squeal.*

Then my mother outside the cottage. *Courage, Comte. You will have your prize.*

Something turned in my head like a key in a lock and now I was truly frightened.

I was the prize they were talking about!

"My mother brought me here to marry me to the *comte*," I whispered.

Evelyn went the colour of marble. "Dear God, child," she said. "I believe you have it." She paused. "But what of Suckley?"

The words tumbled out of my mouth.

"Suckley's a decoy. My mother used him to disguise Landemer's visit to Hawkstone." I shuddered as I remembered the comte's snide questions and pale eyes. "Landemer came to look me over like a breeding cow."

"Bolton was asking for Suckley," said Evelyn thoughtfully. "Do you know where he is?"

I shook my head. "Suckley's not here and from what I heard my mother say to the comte, whatever they have been planning will take place tomorrow."

Evelyn's eyes opened wide. "I must send word," she said under her breath. Then half to herself, she muttered, "Sam should be with us by now."

My insides flipped over at the mention of his voice.

Suddenly half a dozen monkeys swarmed up the side of the fountain and one of them grabbed at Evelyn's sleeve. She tried to bat it away, but it jumped on her shoulder. She screamed and poked it with her fan.

I didn't move as it leaped from her shoulder to mine. All my life, I'd wanted to see a real monkey, but now I was face to face with one, all I could think of was Sam.

The monkey peered at me with bright, clever eyes. He stank worse than a foxhole.

Distractedly, I put out a finger to feel his fur.

"Don't touch him!" shrieked Evelyn. "They bite!"

The monkey started at the sound of her voice then quick as a snake, he reached out a paw and snatched the agate brooch from the front of my dress.

"Give that back," I shouted, and tried to grab the brooch from him. But it was too late. He leaped over to the other side of the fountain, gave me a long look from his clever eyes and tossed the brooch into the water.

"A thousand pardons, lady!" A man with dark skin, wearing a turban and baggy trousers like a Turkish merchant, ran up to me. He had bells on his fingers and two hooped gold earrings in his ears. He knelt before me as if he was praying, then he looked up at me through his fingers.

I gasped. This was no ordinary Turk. The violet eyes I dreamed of night after night sparkled out of his tanned, brown face.

"Tonight," whispered Sam, "we'll dance the saltarello."

And before I could speak, he was gone again, ambling across the garden and shaking the bells on his fingers with the troupe of monkeys dancing behind him.

Chapter Seventeen

The next four hours went as slowly as sugar syrup poured from a cold pitcher. Finally, it was time for the banquet to begin and I made my own way into the Great Hall. As I stood in the doorway, waiting my turn to go in, my mother appeared unexpectedly and stopped me. "You are flushed, daughter," she said, peering closely at my face. "Has something discomfited you? I would have your best manners in front of our Queen."

Knowing Sam was somewhere in the house gave me fresh strength. "I am confused, Mother," I replied, making my voice sound meek. "Lord Suckley is not to be found and I hear no mention in this house of the marriage you settled between us." I held on to my nerve. "You and I have not spoken since my arrival. I am worried that I have upset you in some way."

My mother glared at me with her goat eyes. "Don't play the fool with me, child. Where is the brooch I sent you?"

My stomach tightened as it used to when I was a child.

"A monkey dropped it into the fountain, Mother," I replied.

We looked at each other and I did not let my eyes slide away. She could no longer bully me.

Uncle Charles walked past and bowed with the smallest movement of his head. I called out to him because it was the only way to get away from the poison in my mother's eyes.

He stopped reluctantly and came over to us.

"Dear Charles," said my mother, holding out her hand to be kissed. "I had hoped to speak with you sooner. I was saddened to hear of Frances' death." She seemed to choose her words carefully. "She was a good wife to you."

My uncle's face was impassive and he let my mother's hand drop from his. "Emerald was with her when she died," he said. I heard an edge to his voice. He was telling her I knew the truth about Arabella.

There was no sign in my mother's face that she understood what he said. Not even the flicker of an eyelid. "The Queen joins us for dancing," she said coldly. She bowed and left us, her stiff, purple skirts rustling as she went.

"Be on your guard, dear one," whispered my uncle. "She means to harm you."

I knew he was right. I put my arm through his and prayed that Sam would come sooner than he promised.

All I could eat at supper was a salad of samphire and sugared lemons. Around me people stuffed courses of tench and venison and swan into their mouths and talked of the price of peppercorns and how cuffs were so long, it was impossible to keep them clean. I nodded and smiled. If I was asked who I was, I gave my name and didn't mention my mother.

When the trenchers were cleared away and the knives and serving spoons that belonged to the house were gathered up, Jane Three knelt beside me with a bowl of hot water. She held out a clean napkin. "Mistress?"

I dipped my hands into the hot water and wiped the sticky lemon juice off my fingers. I knew she had recognised me.

"Not a word, as you love your Queen," I said in a low voice.

Jane Three gazed at me with a look of pure delight. "Not a word, miss," she whispered.

I stood up from the bench as the houseboys carefully set aside the leftovers to feed the kitchen. Then they rubbed down the long tables and folded them against the wall. There was a tense, expectant feeling in the room as the boys left and liveried servants began to set up music stands in a corner.

I followed a group of ladies out of the big doors and into the garden for some fresh air. Everyone was hot and full of food, and some ladies were clearly regretting the horn busks they had put down the front of their corsets to make their stomachs look flat. It was easier for the men. Several of them had already wandered away and now they stood at the edges of the garden with their backs to the crowd while they unbuttoned and made water on the grass.

I heard John Bolton's voice above the rest. He was propped up against a stone mermaid, talking as if he'd already had too much wine. I turned away before he noticed me.

A chirping whistle came from behind a hedge clipped to look like a peacock with a full fan of feathers. The hairs on the back of my neck stood on end. Meg was the only person who whistled like that. And then she was in front of me, her face smeared with bootblack, dressed in baggy trousers and a striped vest.

Meg did a backflip and shook the bells she was wearing on her wrist. "Where's Marchand?" she sang in a high, silly voice.

I burst out laughing. She had changed herself into a circus child. It was the perfect disguise, just as it had been for Sam.

"Tell Sam that Marchand is Comte Landemer," I sang, clapping my hands. "They're trying to make me marry him."

"Where? Where? Where?" trilled Meg.

"In the cottage with the weather vane."

Meg let out a whoop and cartwheeled past me, back through the hedge where she had come from.

When I turned around, everyone in the garden was looking up at the roof of the house. No one would have paid much attention to a circus child doing somersaults – she was just one of the entertainers roaming the grounds. But now she could tell Sam about Landemer and he would work out the rest. I felt dizzy with relief and joined the others, craning my head to see what was about to happen.

A line of trumpeters appeared above us. On either side of them, a dozen servants in scarlet livery held up fluttering banners hung with tassels. The sun was setting and flashed pink and gold in the windows of the house.

The crowd on the lawn was getting bigger and more excited and a sense of anticipation clutched at my stomach. We all knew that at any moment, we would see the Queen.

There was huge *bang* and a plume of sparks shot up into the sky. Explosion followed explosion. Soon the air was thick with smoke and the stink of sulphur and bits of flaming fireworks drifted like snowflakes all around us.

The trumpeters raised their instruments to their lips and the air trembled with their music. When it seemed like their lungs would surely burst, there was an ear-splitting crescendo and a horseshoe of servants stepped forward, each one holding up a flaming torch.

I gasped like everyone around me.

In the centre of the horseshoe a figure appeared, dressed from head to toe in a brilliant, silver gown that glittered like diamonds.

The Queen.

The crowd roared. The Queen lifted her arms into the air and the white cloak fixed to her shoulders spread out on either side of her like a pair of wings.

I have never heard such a frenzied cry as the one we all made. It could have split the sky. When I thought of it later, we sounded like wild things.

I felt myself being jostled and pushed towards the house, and moved sideways to get away from the crush around the door. I found myself outside a window looking into the Great Hall.

A dais with a throne and piles of cushions had been set up at the far end of the room. Royal musicians dressed in a livery of scarlet and gold were standing in the corner, tuning their instruments. A man with a recorder was nervously chewing his fingernails and spitting out bits on the floor.

I thought of the last time I had danced the saltarello and leaned against a stone lintel to stop my heart hammering. I remembered how Sam had lifted me so I didn't stumble, and the warmth of his breath on my neck. I wanted to be in his arms again so much it hurt.

A man on a horse was trotting slowly down the drive towards the house. The rider was leaning into his saddle, as if he had travelled a very long way. As he came into the light of the brazier, I saw his face.

It was Richard.

A stable boy rushed out to take the reins as Richard swung out of his saddle and down on to the grass. The boy led the horse away.

"Richard!" I cried, throwing my arms round him. "I'm *so* glad to see you."

"And I you, sister!" He held me in his arms, and I breathed in his scent of leather and horse. "I've ridden all the way from Portsmouth and I'm ready to drop." He pulled back and smiled at me. "'Strewth, you're looking beautiful, Emerald. I wouldn't have known you if you hadn't called."

"Nonsense, brother," I replied. "Your eyes are full of grit from the road."

Richard rolled his eyes the way he always did when we talked this way and rubbed his hand over his face. "Have you seen our mother?"

I nodded.

"How is she?"

When I didn't reply at once, Richard frowned and peered into my face. "What is it, sister?"

I didn't know where to begin. "This is a bad place, Richard," I said in a low voice. "Nothing is as I expected."

I put my arm through his and led him away from the house towards a stone bench outside the dairy. There I sat him down and told him as much as I could about Arabella and Suckley and our mother.

"So where *is* Arabella?" asked Richard at last. "She hasn't replied to any of my letters." He sounded peeved. "I've been half mad with worry." He sighed deeply. "I couldn't tell you at Hawkstone, sister, but Arabella and I plan to marry this summer."

"I've told you what I know," I said, trying hard to keep my temper. He didn't ask or seem to care about the marriage that had been planned for me. "Arabella disappeared this morning. Hetty thinks she has gone back to London."

"Charles will know where she is," said Richard, as though dismissing what I had just said.

"No," I said. "Uncle Charles came to me this morning. He and Arabella have had some kind of disagreement. He is worried sick about her. None of us know where she is."

"Have you asked our mother?" demanded Richard.

"Why would she care?" I asked.

"God's death!" cried Richard. "What is going on here?" There was a note in his voice that I'd heard before in Arabella's voice and even Uncle Charles'. It was hurt and confusion and despair.

I had been wrong to promise Arabella that I wouldn't tell Richard the truth about our mother. He had every right to know, but I would wait until I saw Arabella again. Then if she didn't tell him, I would.

Suddenly trumpets sounded, and there was the noise of people shouting and cheering again.

I stood up and smoothed down my dress. "The Queen is taking her place in the hall. We can't be late." I held out my hand. "Perhaps Arabella has returned already and I haven't seen her."

Richard put his arm round my shoulder. "Tell me, sister, do you think a mustard-coloured doublet and black hose

229

will pass as fine clothes for Her Highness? They've had three days in the saddle, but I've little else with me than a clean shirt."

"You'll be fine," I said, but I wasn't thinking about Richard's clothes. I was thinking about Sam.

Chapter Eighteen

The musicians were playing a gavotte as Richard and I took our places in the crowded hall. Nobody greeted him because no one knew him. Besides, everyone's eyes were on the woman dressed in silver who sat straight-backed in front of us, her gaunt, sharp-eyed face looking firmly ahead. In one hand she held a fan and in the other a fine, white stick, which she tapped on the arm of her chair to keep time to the slow, rhythmic chords of the lute.

Behind her, my mother stood with her husband. It was only the second time I'd seen Henry of Orgon since our brief introduction in the hall. He stood patiently with an absent expression on his face as if the real world was going on inside his head. Beside him, my mother was a coiled spring.

The Queen waved a jewelled hand. Henry of Orgon bowed and led my mother on to the floor.

To my surprise, they danced well together, her steps even and measured. But she moved with the insistence of a man, not the lightness of a woman, and none of her gestures were graceful or witty.

I felt Richard shift from foot to foot as my mother came towards us and I knew the mix of dread and hope he was feeling. Like me, he hadn't seen her for seven years. I heard him take a breath when they were barely an arm's stretch away.

Richard opened his mouth to greet her. But my mother only stared at him. Then she turned her head and danced away.

At that moment, Uncle Charles strode up to us, his arms held out in front of him. "Richard! My dear man!"

He hugged Richard close. Richard took a moment to collect himself, then hugged our uncle back.

"I thought you were in Lisbon," said Uncle Charles, as they drew apart.

"Lisbon?" spluttered Richard. "We've been nowhere near Portugal. Why would you think that?" He turned to me with a look on his face which said more than words. "Arabella must have told you?"

I shook my head. I had a horrible sense something dreadful was about to happen.

"I gave my news to Arabella," explained Richard to Charles. He reddened. "We'd agreed…" His face said everything.

My uncle's eyes bulged with disbelief. "Agreed *what*, sir?" he demanded.

Richard started as if he had been struck in the face. Then he pulled himself together and said, "I have been three days in the saddle to see your daughter. I cannot speak what is on my mind until then."

My uncle's face went grey. I wished there was something I could say to help him, but there was nothing. It was too late.

Richard stared at me as if he was drowning and I turned away.

"Pray, excuse me, gentlemen." Evelyn of Lambeth appeared at our side. She looked between the two men and let her eyes drop. To my amazement I realised she must have understood what had happened. And the only way that could be, was if Arabella had told her.

I made rapid introductions, then Evelyn said, "I have news from Arabella."

"When did you speak with her?" demanded Richard. "Where is she?"

Evelyn looked calmly at his angry face. "I cannot tell you that, sir. She swore me to secrecy."

"Poppycock!" snapped Richard.

"Richard, please!" I said. "Evelyn is a good friend."

"What is your news, madam?" asked Charles. "We are all confounded."

We stood in uncomfortable silence as Evelyn said, "Arabella would have you all know she is well, but she has business in Oxford, and will stay there the night. She is sorry for any worry she has caused."

Evelyn bowed at Richard. "A pleasure to make your acquaintance, sir," she said, and left.

"Who was that woman?" demanded Richard. "How can she know where Arabella is when no one else does?" He turned angrily to me. "What are you hiding, sister? I know you think little of Arabella."

Tears gathered in my eyes as I saw my uncle's face crumple with despair.

"You know *nothing,* Richard," I said in a hard, furious voice. I could hardly bear to keep Arabella's secret any longer. "But by God you'll soon find out!"

I pushed through the crowded room towards the stairs. Every nerve in my body was burning, and my bones felt ready to crack. I couldn't wait for Sam another minute.

Someone grabbed me by the arm from behind. I knew it wasn't Sam because the fingers pressed hard on my skin, and I felt the sharpness of fingernails digging into me. I tried to pull my arm away, but the grip didn't loosen. Only Suckley would behave as oafishly as that.

A red storm burst in my head. If I'd had a knife, I would have stabbed him. As it was, I had a long, pearl-headed hairpin. I drew it out of my hair with my right hand and plunged it into the hand that held me.

"God's teeth!" John Bolton cried out.

I turned and saw blood seeping from his wrist on to the white lace of his cuff. His eyes were two chips of yellow glass in his sweaty face. "You'll regret that, madam," he snarled. "You mother will be informed."

"Tell my mother what you like, sir," I snapped. "Get out of my way."

Bolton lunged towards me, making to grab my hand. Then a figure I hadn't noticed before stepped between us.

Sam!

With a quick movement of his foot, Sam stamped on Bolton's feet. Then he put his lips to my ear. "How fierce you have become, my darling! I swear I am quite terrified of you."

As Bolton stamped off nursing his bleeding wrist, the players began a saltarello.

Sam put his arm through mine and we walked together into the hall with the bright, joyful music ringing in our eyes.

We looked into each other's eyes for an instant then we set off twirling and skipping the length of the room.

Everyone was watching us, but I didn't care. Sam was beside me now. No one could hurt me any more.

Or so I thought at the time.

Chapter Nineteen

"'Strewth, miss," said Sarah. "It ain't many as can have looked into the Queen's face twice in two days." She loosened my corset and untied the underskirt that was stiffened with circles of rope. It was a relief to feel the weight of them drop to the floor. "D'you think she recognised you?"

"I'm not sure," I replied. I tugged at my garters and rolled down my silk stockings. "I was so nervous both times, I can hardly remember."

But I did remember and even thinking about it made my stomach crawl with butterflies all over again.

When the saltarello had finished, Sam had whispered, "I love you," and disappeared into the crowd. Before I could move to the edge of the room, a royal servant came up to me. Everyone around me immediately stopped talking. It was so quiet, I could hear the rustle of skirts and the whisper of fans.

"Her Majesty would speak to you, madam," he said.

I followed him up the dais to where my mother and

Henry of Orgon sat on low stools either side of the Queen.

The Queen herself was sitting on a fine chair with tall candlesticks set all around her. The silver gown she wore glittered in the light and her hair was covered with a lace veil sewn with diamonds. She leaned back on her chair, one hand resting on the wooden arm. The ruby on her forefinger was the size of a blackbird's egg.

I swept a deep curtsey in front of her, praying she wouldn't remember the grubby boy who had given her a bunch of flowers.

"You are an excellent dancer, child," said the Queen, smiling. "It was a pleasure to watch you." Her eyes looked straight through me, just as they had done before, and if she knew who I was, she didn't show it. But even though my legs were shaking and my mind spun like a child's top, this time I wasn't terrified.

I said, "Your Majesty does me a great honour."

"No, my dear," said the Queen, "you do me an honour. It isn't often I see such grace and command of the steps." She leaned forward. "I sent my servant because I do not know your name."

My eyes slid sideways to my mother's face. It could have been made of rock, but the fury underneath it bubbled like lava. It was clearly not part of her plan that I should bring such attention to myself.

The Queen followed my gaze and a flicker of curiosity passed over her face.

"My name is Emerald St John, Your Majesty." I turned away from my mother's gaze. I didn't care any more. "I am Lady Millicent's daughter."

The curiosity on the Queen's face deepened and she raised her eyebrows a fraction.

"You hide your treasure carefully, madam," she said, turning to my mother.

My mother bowed her head as if her neck was made of glass. "If it please Your Majesty, it was my intention to present my daughter to you at the banquet, tomorrow." She tried to soften the look in her eyes, but it didn't work. Then she said, as if to explain the spectacle I had made of myself, "Emerald was always a spirited child."

"How consoling, Lady Millicent," replied the Queen with the faintest edge to her voice. "The same was said of me as a young girl."

She turned back to me and rested a skinny finger on my sleeve. "You have unusual eyes, my dear. Apart from dancing skills, have you any other unusual accomplishments?"

"Emerald lives in Wales, Majesty," said my mother quickly. "An almanac and a Bible are her reading."

The Queen ignored her. "Your eyes tell me a different story," she said, looking at me. "What is the truth?"

"I'd wager your mother could have murdered you then and there," cried Sarah, grinning.

I grinned back. "My mother would have stabbed me if she'd had a dagger at her side."

Sarah picked up a brush and pulled it through my hair. "So what did you tell the Queen?"

"I told her the truth," I replied. "I said that I could speak three languages and read Latin fluently. That thanks to my aunt I know herbs and their remedies and thanks to my father I can catch anything that swims."

Sarah groaned with delight. "How did the Queen reply?"

"She asked me if there was anything I *couldn't* do."

I laughed as I remembered the conversation.

"I'm stupid with cards, Your Majesty," I told her. "I don't like gambling and my conversation is mostly about vegetables."

"Gold is only dull because it lacks polishing," replied the Queen.

She turned to my mother. "Pray you, madam, send this daughter of yours to my ladies in the morning. She shall attend me tomorrow."

The Queen tapped her finger on my wrist. "Tell me, who was your partner for the saltarello?"

There was no time to make up a story, and I didn't want to. "It was Viscount Pemberton, Your Highness," I said. "He's a friend of my brother Richard and a fellow sailor on *The Pigeon*."

"Pemberton," said the Queen slowly. "I have heard of him. He is able and intelligent." She leaned forward and I smelled orange peel on her breath. "Have a care, mistress. The fellow is in love with you."

My mother must have heard because she gasped and her hand flew to her throat.

The Queen frowned then she stood up and the music stopped. "My thanks for an engaging evening, Lady Millicent," she said.

My mother curtsied. She had recovered herself, but I felt she would have spat at me if she could.

Suddenly I remembered my uncle's warning. *She means to harm you.* And a shiver of fear went through me.

Once again, it was as if the Queen was reading my mind. "Come, child." She took my arm and didn't look back at my mother. "You may walk with me to my chamber. I would like some fresh air."

"Oh, miss!" said Sarah admiringly. "Did Lord Sam see you with Her Majesty?"

"No. We'd made our plan and he had letters to write to London." I stood up. I was wearing Sarah's servant dress over three layers of clothes. Her grey apron with the Hawkstone rose was tied loosely round my waist. "Do I look enough like you?"

Sarah laughed. "I'd say you're bulky enough now." She pulled up the wings of my collar so that they were almost touching my chin. "Keep your eyes on the ground and you might get away with it." She handed me a pair of clogs. "Best have a try with these before you go."

I pushed my feet into the heavy wooden shoes. I hadn't

worn clogs since I was a child and, when I walked around the room, they felt clumsy and heavy.

Sarah tied a folded, cream-coloured cap over my head and pulled the sides down over my ears. Then she put a bucket in front of me. "If anyone stops you, this is your excuse. No one will question a servant fetching water for her mistress."

I stared at the bucket. My disguise was part of the plan Sam had explained to me as we danced. I was to meet him in the well yard. He'd be dressed like a laundry man. The well yard was a busy place.

"We'll just be two servants talking. No one will notice us."

At the time, his idea had seemed like an exciting adventure. It would give us time to talk, and secretly I wanted to surprise him with a kiss like the one I'd given him at Hawkstone. But now I wasn't sure. I was desperate to see him, but terrified in case something went wrong. It would be foolish to underestimate my mother's malice and her plan to marry me off to Landemer.

Sarah touched my arm. "Everything will go well," she said. "I'm sure of it." She pointed to the clogs. "Try not to run."

The clock struck nine as I made my way down the stairs to the bottom of the house. Every corridor was crowded with servants who were tired or drunk or both. I cursed myself for being so clumsy in Sarah's clogs. It was hard not to step on the ones who had given up and were slumped against the wall, half asleep.

241

"The well yard's got water in barrels in the far corner," Sarah had told me. "There'll be others waiting. When it's your turn, dip your bucket in quick and don't spill any. There will be cursing and shouting if you do, and someone'll notice."

It turned out the barrels were empty because there weren't enough water boys to draw water from the well. Some said to fill up in the stream and that I was a fool for waiting in the yard, but I told them I was afraid of the mooncalf and they left me alone.

There was a long line for the well, but I was sure that Sam would come before I had to draw my own water. I kept peering in front to see what kind of a knot the others used to tie their bucket on to the rope, and how long they let it drop before turning the handle to pull it up again. But every time I tried to see, someone pushed me back in line.

The clocks struck half past the hour.

"You daft or summat?" said a bleary-eyed woman behind me. She stank of beer and kitchen grease. "Your turn. Get on with it."

A length of wet rope hung down the well like the tail of some dead animal. It was slimy and I almost dropped it, but I got a grip and tied it on to the handle of my bucket with the knot I always used to tie a fly to a line.

I let go and the handle spun around as the bucket plunged out of sight.

When the handle stopped spinning, I tried to pull the

bucket up. But it was so heavy, I could barely do three turns and beads of sweat broke out on my lips. What kind of servant couldn't draw water?

"I'll 'elp you, Sarah." It was Hetty's voice. She must have seen the rose on my apron. I almost dropped the handle. If she recognised me, everything would be lost.

"Thanks." I tucked my head into my collar and hoped my bulky shape and the darkness of the yard would save me. I moved over and Hetty took the handle beside me.

"This is a bad house, Sarah," said Hetty as we pulled at the handle together. "I've never seen the master so doleful."

I grunted in the hope that Hetty would keep talking like she usually did. "Truth is, I's glad I seen ya, cos I's leavin' tomorrow. Mistress sent word."

I looked sideways at Hetty's face. It was pouchy and smudged, as if she'd been crying and wiped her eyes with a sooty handkerchief.

I had to find out what she knew before the bucket came up. "Poor Hetty," I murmured, trying to sound like Sarah. "You've been worried sick, I know. Where's Miss Arabella been?"

"She made me swear," sniffed Hetty. "Told me I'd be in the gutter if I blabbed." She heaved the bucket on to the ground, and water glinted silver in the moonlight. "Gutter or not," she muttered peevishly, "they'll all know tomorrow anyway."

My breath caught in my throat. I knew Hetty. If I asked

too much, she wouldn't tell me. So I said nothing as we lugged the bucket across the muddy yard.

"What riles me," said Hetty after an intake of breath, "is why she said yes to that festering toad."

The hairs on the back of my neck stood up. "What festering toad?"

"Suckley, of course," snapped Hetty. "Miss Arabella's set to marry him."

I dropped my side of the bucket handle and water slopped over both of us.

"Clumsy ninnies!" shouted the same stinking woman who had been behind me at the well. "From London, are ya?" She waved a stubby torch and both of our faces were lit up in the light.

"You!" shouted Hetty in a horrified voice. "What are *you* doing here?"

The old woman peered at us suspiciously.

"Fetching water, you numbskull!" I hissed at Hetty. "Or ain't it allowed?"

"What's up with you two?" demanded the woman.

Hetty realised we were both in a dangerous position. "Leave us be, ya stinking slag," she muttered. "We ain't done nothin' wrong."

"Town sluts," snarled the woman and went on her way. I picked up the empty bucket and tugged Hetty across the yard towards a gap between two stacks of wood.

"Don't tell no one, mistress, please!" Hetty sobbed. "I'll be beggin' for my bread if you do."

"Stop howling," I snapped. "You'll get us noticed."

I pushed her into the gap and went in after.

Hetty slumped on to the ground and put her head in her hands. "I'd never have said nothing if I'd known it was you," she moaned. "I don't understand. It was you 'e was to marry, not Miss Arabella."

I sat down beside her and gave her one of the sweetmeats I'd hidden in my apron for Sam. I'd never liked Hetty, but now I felt sorry for her. "You're right. This is a bad place, Hetty."

I handed her another sweetmeat. "Tell me what happened."

Hetty eyed me suspiciously. Then in the shadowy light, I saw her face change. She'd worked out that if she told me what I wanted to know, I'd owe her a favour.

"I weren't to go near 'er chest from the very beginnin'," said Hetty. "All them lovely dresses the master paid for, an' not one did she touch. An' every time I asked, she shouted at me. Then two nights ago, her bed weren't slept in an' in the mornin' she was gone." She sniffed again and wiped her mouth on her sleeve. "Then Lady Lambeth's maid came this morning and fetched some belongings."

"Which ones?"

Hetty picked at her nose. "'Ow should I know? I wasn't there."

"But you know what's missing," I said. "Tell me, Hetty."

"The ring box, some linen and her embroidered cap

245

and shawl," said Hetty. "My guess is she'd planned to wear 'em in front of the priest."

She stood up and her fat ferret face looked greasy and tired. "That's all I know, miss," she said, and then she ran off without looking back.

I leaned against the cut wood and breathed in its smell of earth and resin. I wanted to cry for Arabella, but I couldn't. I knew why she had married Suckley, but it was impossible to imagine two people who hated each other more.

But I was sure my mother had no idea what Suckley had done.

The clock struck ten and I made my way back across the yard towards the well. It was still warm. Everywhere there were bonfires, and the sound of voices in the dark.

A gloved hand took me by the wrist and pulled me through a door. At first I thought it was Sam. Then Evelyn of Lambeth's voice hissed in my ear. "Not a word, on your life!"

I looked through the half-open door on to the moonlit yard. No one was waiting for the well any more and what servants were still up were sitting in groups around fires or curled up in dark corners for the night.

Then my heart stopped. A young woman dressed in my azure gown stepped hesitantly out of the back door into the yard. A long cloak was wrapped round her shoulders and her face was hidden in a hood. I watched as she made her way towards the stables.

At that moment, two men jumped out of the shadows. I opened my mouth to scream, but Evelyn clamped her glove over my lips.

Then I watched in horror as the men put a sack over the girl's head and dragged her away.

Chapter Twenty

Meg plucked at my sleeve and held out a mug of hot milk. "Don't cry so, miss! You're safe. It's you they wants, not 'er. That's what Red Hat said." Meg folded her arms. "Sarah knew you'd be all a-fluster." She mimicked Sarah's voice. "*You tell her, Meg. 'Tis my decision and I've decided. An' I'll do me best with keeping mud off the gown.*"

I wiped my nose and tried to smile. "She didn't say that about the gown, Meg."

"All right, she didn't," admitted Meg. "But she warned me as there'd be a lot of snivelling from you." She held up a piece of folded paper. "'Ere – an' don't soak it through so's you can't read it."

"Meg!" I protested. "I've never heard such talk! Who gave you that note?"

"Red Hat," said Meg, handing it to me. "Said you was to read it as soon as you was yerself again. So's I could explain."

I opened the note and saw Sam's writing.

Darling. Do not meet me in any guise. Landemer means to

kidnap you and take you before a priest. I'll be near at all times. Be brave, my love. Sam

"Seems everyone wants to marry you, don't it, miss?" Meg beamed at me and stuffed a jellied fruit in her mouth.

"Whose idea was it to dress up as me?" I asked.

"Wait!" cried Meg. "It's my story!" She sat down cross-legged at the end of the bed and began to talk.

"It were Sarah that thought it," said Meg. "Red Hat said she's never met one as smart as her. Exceptin' you, miss. Called you a jewel, she did."

I rubbed my hand over my face and felt tears leak through my fingers. Meg moved up beside me.

"It were like this, miss," she said. "Only swear you won't sniff."

I sniffed and nodded.

"So Sarah an' me is mendin' stuff," said Meg. "An' Red Hat knocks at the door to see you. She looks all flustered, but you ain't here only me 'n' Sarah, like I said. At first no one says nuffin'. Then Sarah tells Red Hat that you's gone to the yard to meet Sam which she let out cos you said somethin' to her about Red Hat being a good 'un."

Meg threw out her arms. "'So,' says Red Hat, 'what's to be done?' An' she explains the note 'n' all. An' I says, 'bad enough a maggoty ape after my mistress, now it's a garlic-gulpin' dog'. Of course, Sarah gives me a bit of a look," said Meg, giggling. "But I know she agrees. That's when she sees your gown. 'What about this?' she says. 'I'll dress up as the mistress and we'll flush 'em out like rabbits.'"

In my mind's eye, I saw a man throw a sack over Sarah's head and drag her into the night. It made me want to howl all over again.

"Who… who's going to rescue her?" I stammered.

"Mr Richard," replied Meg. "Red Hat said those French dogs would take you to some cottage with a windy vane." Her eyes gleamed. "I'd say he and Sam are choppin' 'em up right now." She patted my arm. "Sarah'll be safe, miss. Red Hat promised."

I lay back on my pillows. Every bone in my body ached. "Arabella is betrothed to Suckley," I murmured. I wanted to tell somebody before I fell asleep.

Meg made a noise like a turkey with a stone stuck in its gizzard.

"That's *disgustin'*!" she cried. She tipped her head on one side. "Beggin' your favour, miss…"

"What?"

"If you's still asleep, can it be me that tells Sarah?"

I was so tired I patted the bed instead of her knee. "Yes, Meg, of course."

A blackbird woke me before dawn. The room was still dark, but I could make out the shape of Sarah asleep on a pallet in the corner by the fireplace. There was no sign of Meg.

Usually I thank God for the world He created, not for the people He put in it. But on that shadowy morning, I thanked Him with all my heart that Sarah was safe, and I prayed that He would watch over all of us on the day that was ahead.

I slid out of bed and opened the shutters. Already the land around the house was crawling with people. Below in the garden, servants were raking gravel. I stood and looked at the meadows and fields stretching away to the forest and the hills beyond. Ragged ribbons of mist floated in the valleys, and a huge yellow sun was already climbing through the clouds. It was going to be another hot, blue day.

In the corner of my eye I saw something move and I laughed out loud. Two monkeys were sitting on the edge of the fountain washing their faces in the water.

Sarah stirred and I went over to her.

"Gracious, miss," she said, still half asleep. "Imagine you being out of your bed instead of me."

"Imagine you being kidnapped instead of me." I took her hand and held it. "Thank God you are safe, Sarah." I bit my lip, determined not to snivel, as Meg would have put it. "Did they hurt you?"

"Not in the slightest." Sarah sat up and untied her nightcap. "I had the sack over my head right to the end. It was Richard who took it off. At least, I think it was him, but he and Sam were wearing masks so they couldn't be recognised." She laughed and her eyes shone. "You should have seen those villains' faces when they saw they'd got the wrong woman!"

I shuddered. I wanted to laugh with her, but I couldn't

251

get the idea out of my head that if it *had* been me, I would be married to Comte Landemer by now.

Sarah looked at my white face and read my thoughts. "Don't fret, miss. It weren't you, it were me, and it's over with. Sam said they were Marchand's men. Or whatever he's called."

"Landemer," I said. "Did Meg tell you about Arabella?"

Sarah nodded. "I'm sorry for her, miss. But she's done the right thing by the child she's carrying."

I knew it was the truth. Even so, it seemed cruel that Arabella had ruined her life through one stupid mistake. She of all people deserved a second chance.

The door flung open and Meg stood in the middle of the room. She held a basket over one arm and she looked as if she was going to explode. "They're sayin' those Frenchmen was robbers, miss," she cried. "An' that 'er ladyship's had 'em cuffed about the head somethin' dreadful and that they's been locked in a cage." She put the basket down on the table. "This were outside the door, miss. It's got peaches and cherry cake, too."

Something snapped inside me. "For heaven's sake, shut up, Meg!"

Meg's face crumpled. "I's only tellin' you, miss," she said. "Eyes an' ears, you said." From the corner of my eye, I could see Sarah waving her away.

I took a breath. "I'm sorry, Meg. Find Lady Lambeth's maidservant and say thank you. I'd say our breakfast came from her."

Meg's face lit up like a candle. "Anythin' else, miss?"

"Have a peach and some cherry cake."

When we were on our own, Sarah said, "Sam and Richard didn't beat up those villains, mistress. They left them trussed up like turkeys." She tied on the apron that I'd worn last night. "I'd say it was your mother's doing to cover her tracks."

I thought for a moment. "So if my mother's covering her tracks, Landemer will be covering his, too." I ran my hands through my hair. "I'm trying to get this straight," I said, half to her and half to myself. "When I see my mother and Landemer today, they are going to pretend that nothing's wrong."

Sarah began to lay out my clothes. "They can hardly admit to a bungled kidnap."

I looked at Sarah. There was no point in secrets now. "Sam says there is a plot to poison the Queen," I said. "That's why we've all been invited here at the same time."

I had expected Sarah to gasp, but she said in a matter-of-fact voice, "If that's so, there's only one wicked enough to think it up and one stupid enough to do her bidding."

She held my gaze.

"My mother and Suckley," I said.

As I spoke, my heart began to bang so hard in my chest, I could hardly breathe. "Dear God, Sarah," I muttered. "How can I stop them?"

Sarah jerked her head and shook out a striped green-and-white skirt with a matching gown and sleeves.

253

"Beggin' your pardon, miss. If there's a plot to kill the Queen, it's up to Sam to stop them."

"But how will he know when they plan to do it?"

Sarah looked at me steadily. "He'll have figured it out just like we have. You've got enough to think about with Molly."

I felt a sharp, edgy pain in my stomach and I realised I was hungry. I pulled the linen cloth from the basket and saw a folded piece of paper with my name on it. I recognised the writing immediately. It wasn't Evelyn who had sent the basket, it was Uncle Charles.

I opened the note.

I have told Richard everything. Our prayers are with you. Charles

"Richard knows about Arabella," I said. "Uncle Charles told him."

"What about Suckley's child?" asked Sarah.

"No one knows about that."

I looked down at my uncle's writing again and thanked him in my heart. At least now, when Richard found out about Arabella's marriage, he would know why she hadn't married him. Even if he didn't understand why she had chosen Suckley. I found myself hoping that Arabella would have the courage to tell Richard the truth. It would hurt him, and no doubt he would be disgusted with her, but it would be an end to it. More and more, I was beginning to understand that we had to put a stop to the lies that had taken over, or they would poison us just as they'd poisoned the lives before ours.

I showed Sarah the letter.

"It was the least he could do," she said, putting her chin in the air. She took out the cherry cake and put it on the table with the peaches. "Eat up, mistress. It's going to be a long day for you."

"It's going to be a long day for everyone," I said.

There was a bottle of grape juice in the basket. I opened it with my penknife and poured it into two mugs. "What's the toast, Sarah?" I handed her a mug.

Sarah's eyes went over to a pair of black satin breeches, which were laid out beside my petticoat. "To God's will in all things."

We held each other's gaze. The time had come at last and I didn't know whether I was exhilarated or terrified.

I drank down the clear, sweet liquid and saw the words in Sam's letter.

Be brave, my love.

Three hours later, after a picnic at which I ate nothing, I was seated beside the Queen, looking down over the bear pit. Since I had joined her retinue that morning, it had been like stepping through a mirror into another world. Everything that happened around us seemed unreal. It was hard to imagine that the men and women who bowed and curtsied and brought her gifts were made of the same flesh and blood as we were. Even their voices sounded like the chatter of birdsong.

A group of musicians stood in the middle of the pit

playing their fiddles. As far as I was concerned, they might as well have been sharpening knives on a whetstone.

The Queen tapped my knee with her fan. I was getting used to the white paste on her face and her rouged cheeks with a beauty spot drawn under each cheekbone. It was like looking at a painted skull.

"Do you follow the hunt?" she asked.

I knew by now that the Queen never asked a question for no reason and something prickled on the edge of my mind. "I ride for sport, Majesty," I replied. "Not for the chase and the kill."

"There is a hunt going on in this house, and you are the quarry," said the Queen flatly.

I felt the colour draining from my face. How could she know?

"Don't look so surprised, child," said the Queen. "I have a hunter's instincts. And I learned them a long time ago."

Trumpets sounded, and I saw my mother and Henry of Orgon come slowly through the arch that led into the bear pit. I felt the Queen stiffen beside me. It had been announced that morning that my mother was indisposed and unable to be present at the day's festivities. Her chair had been left empty at the banquet earlier, and there was talk of a physician being summoned.

Now she walked slowly, on the arm of her husband, with a stick in her free hand. Her skin was grey, as if she had been sick to her stomach all night. When the two of

256

them stopped to acknowledge the Queen's presence, her eyes were two black holes above a red gash of a mouth.

I looked away. I didn't want her to read anything from my face. All she could know was that Landemer's thugs had kidnapped the wrong woman and that she had then been rescued by two men wearing masks. I shivered despite myself, wondering if she had been watching while the French kidnappers were questioned and beaten.

I looked at the rows of people standing and sitting around the pit, but there was no sign of Sam or Richard. Then, to my horror, Lord Suckley was standing in front of us.

I gasped despite myself and Suckley must have heard me because he threw me a look of pure hatred.

"My Lord Suckley," said the Queen in an icy voice. "I am surprised to see you. Usually when a courtier marries one of my ladies, he asks for my permission."

"Majesty," spluttered Suckley. He pointed to me. "This child—"

"Fie, Suckley!" interrupted the Queen, laughing at his dark face. "Surely you don't think Emerald spies for me?" She tipped her head sideways. "I have eyes and ears in every place."

"I beg your forgiveness, Majesty," cried Suckley in a pitiful voice. He looked like a rat trapped in a corner, and he stopped, not knowing what to say next. "It was not my intention – that is to say, I am come to serve you. If it pleases you, Majesty."

The Queen seemed to be enjoying herself. "What have you done with your bride, Suckley? Surely Arabella Mount is not frightened to present herself to me? She was always a splendid talker when she was put to it."

I could not believe what I was hearing. How could the Queen have learned so much since yesterday evening? The answer was given to me, even as I thought it.

On the other side of the pit, Evelyn of Lambeth took her place in the front row. Even though I couldn't see her face, I knew she was looking at me. It was she who had told the Queen. As I watched courtiers on either side make way for her, I began to realise that Sam's mother was very well connected indeed. And now I understood why he had been prepared to let me come to Bleathwood on my own.

To my astonishment, I saw Arabella appear in the back row with her father. They made their way down to where Evelyn was sitting. Again, at Evelyn's nod, room was made for them. I watched my uncle show Arabella to her seat. There was something tender about his movements and it made me think that Arabella had told her father everything.

Cymbals clashed and there was a yell from the crowd. The Queen lost interest in Suckley and leaned forward.

A man strode into the middle of the pit leading three mastiffs on the end of a rope. The dogs howled and snarled and pulled at their collars. He knocked a stake into the ground with a hammer and tied the rope round it. Then he turned and bowed to the Queen.

The Queen leaned forward with her lips parted. "Do you come with a bear, sir?" she cried out in her piercing voice.

"I come with two, Your Majesty," shouted the man.

"How can that be?" demanded the Queen. "We only brought one!"

"Compliments of Lady Millicent," shouted the man. His smile was all teeth in his dark face. "A young 'un for your pleasure."

Even though it was what I had prepared for, hearing the crowd's roar of approval made me sick to my stomach. Suckley turned to me and whispered under his breath, "I hope the dogs get her guts."

Later, I thought that I would have fainted had it not been for Suckley. As it was, the sound of his voice set me on fire with rage. "Your guts will come first, sir," I hissed at him.

His lips twisted like live things. "You betrayed me," he snarled.

I stared at him. "No, sir," I said, with all of the menace I could bring to my voice. "You betrayed yourself."

The man cracked his whip over the dogs. Any minute now, the first bear would be brought in. I stood up to beg leave from the Queen – even though I would have gone whether she let me go or not.

I didn't have to ask. The Queen's eyes flickered across Suckley's face and I saw the imperceptible nod of her head.

Had she heard what Suckley said? Did she know about Molly? I'll never know. As I pushed my way through the crowds, I saw a man with a feather in his cap and a red tunic, leading a mangy bear into the pit. The mastiffs went wild.

I gathered my skirts and climbed the steep steps. I had to find Molly before the bear keeper got there first.

Chapter Twenty-one

"I'll undo yer laces, miss!" Meg was standing on a box behind the walls of the bear pit. "Sarah says you'll never get yer breeches on by yer own."

Meg tugged and pulled at the fastenings of my dress while I unhooked my sleeves and untied my petticoat. I didn't care who was watching. A few minutes later, I stood in a pair of black satin breeches with a gold waistcoat over my blouse.

"Where's Tom?" I kicked off my slippers and pulled on a pair of long, black boots.

"Over there with the gut bucket." She waved her hand at Tom who was leaning against a tree, staring pointedly at the ground. A bucket swarming with flies was at his feet.

Inside the pit, the noise of the crowd was getting louder, and the dogs were yelping and snarling. A whip cracked and a bear roared, half mad with pain. I twisted my hair into a knot, stuffed it under a black velvet beret and pushed in a pearl-headed pin to hold it in place. Then I pulled on the mask and took a deep breath. I was ready.

We were following the plan we'd made by Tom's camp. He knew about bear pits. He'd been taken to them as a boy. "Molly'll be chained up, miss, waitin' her turn. I'll smash the lock and Meg'll rattle the gut bucket for the dogs. As soon as they comes, I'll rope 'em up and you leads Molly in. Let's go."

Tom hadn't told me what he had in mind for anyone who got in his way, but I soon found out. Two men came at him as we walked to the door that led under the seats and into the pit. He knocked out the first one with a punch and flattened the second with the back of his hand. I wasn't bothered. If I'd had time, I'd have stuck them both with my hairpin for good measure. When I got to Molly, she was trembling with terror. I rubbed her neck and whispered to her until she stopped shaking. As soon as Tom had tied up the dogs, I led her into the bright sunlight of the pit.

The crowd went quiet. The Queen was leaning forward in her chair, watching curiously. The old bear was standing in the middle of the pit, his huge head swinging from side to side as if the dogs were still around him. Blood oozed from his snout and there was a gash in one of his hind legs. I had expected him to snarl, but when he saw Molly he stood still, snuffed the air and whinnied at her.

Molly whinnied in return and pulled at her rope. I couldn't hold her back because she was too strong, so I let her go over to him. They sniffed at each other, and she tried to lick the blood from his snout, but he

262

pushed her away, and I saw that one of his paws had been badly bitten.

"Bring back the dogs!" shouted a voice from the crowd. It was Suckley. He was standing with his hands cupped round his mouth, looking around for approval.

I steeled myself for a bloodthirsty roar, but it didn't come. The crowd had taken to what they saw and wanted to know what would come next. Perhaps it was my costume, or perhaps it was true that most people didn't have the stomach to watch such dreadful cruelty.

Either way, I knew it wouldn't last long. I bowed to the Queen and held both arms in the air.

"Your Majesty! Brave ladies and gentlemen," I shouted in the deepest voice I could manage. "I present Molly, the cleverest bear in England!"

Molly's ears pricked up at the sound of her name. I clapped my hands twice, and we set off round the pit. There was a smattering of applause and my heart leaped in my chest. "God save you, Molly!" I cried. And I led her through the tumbles she had learned on the lower field at Hawkstone.

It was as if the bear pit had become a circus. As Molly showed her tricks, I could sense the crowd willing her on. They wanted fun and something to cheer for. At the same time, I heard the musicians strike up and the sound of fiddles and tambourines mixed with the hot, dusty air. The crowd began to clap and a few people threw flowers. As luck would have it, I caught hold of a bouquet of daisies

263

as it sailed past my head. Everyone laughed as I bowed and tucked the bunch under Molly's collar.

A table with a white cloth had been set in front of the Queen and now my mother and Henry of Orgon moved to sit behind her. I was surprised to see Suckley standing a few feet from my mother's chair. It was a privileged position and he would only have taken it if she had invited him there.

Two servants set out goblets on the table while a third handed Suckley a crystal jug full of wine. I didn't move. It was like watching a tableau performed by some troupe of oddly mixed actors and I couldn't take my eyes off it. Molly turned to me with a puzzled look on her face. I was supposed to be running alongside her. Any minute now, she'd hear my voice and feel the weight of a corn sack as I jumped on to her back. She'd carry me until I shouted and pulled on her rope. Then she'd stop and there would be an apple and a lump of sugar to eat.

Suckley picked up a crystal goblet from the table and began to pour out wine. He looked pompous and self-important and kept turning to my mother, as if he wanted her approval. But my mother never acknowledged him and stared forward as if he wasn't there.

The Queen had no idea of what was going on around her. Her face was alight and she was staring at Molly with the delight of a child.

Then something happened that made me cry out.

Comte Landemer suddenly appeared from the shadows

of a doorway at the back of the stand. He made his way smoothly to a place by my mother's side. For the first time, I looked at Henry of Orgon. He was picking at his seal ring and, like the Queen in front, seemed oblivious of everything around him.

There was no sign of Sam anywhere.

It all happened very slowly. Suckley put down the jug on the table and picked up the goblet. I watched Landemer's face. It was as still as a mask. Beside him, my mother's pallor had gone and there was a warm, greasy look of triumph on her face.

Suddenly I understood. My mother was planning to murder the Queen with poisoned wine – but not by her own hand. Suckley was her stooge, lured to Bleathwood with a promise of a marriage that was never intended to happen. When Suckley had fulfilled his purpose and the Queen lay dying, Landemer would act the loyal servant and run him through with his sword.

At first I couldn't work out what my mother would have to gain from the death of the Queen in her own house. Then I remembered Sam once telling me that power is all about influence and, finally, I understood what he meant.

My mother had long ago switched her allegiance to the Catholic faction and married Henry of Orgon to strengthen that. Her true partner was Comte Landemer who was as ruthless and ambitious as she was. The death of the Queen at Bleathwood, and the assassination of her so-called murderer by Landemer would guarantee my mother's influence in the choice of the Queen's successor. That she had been prepared to sacrifice me to dupe Suckley and betray her own husband and my guardians was truly monstrous, and I wondered again if there was a madness in her.

Even now, when Suckley had proved to be unreliable and the abduction had gone wrong, she carried on as if her own ambition was all that mattered.

All this flashed through my mind as Suckley picked up the goblet of wine and held it out towards the Queen.

There was no time to shout out a warning. The Queen was completely distracted by Molly. There was only one thing I could do. I picked up a stone from the ground. In my mind I was by the river at Hawkstone again, and there was a magpie in the tree. I prayed for a true aim and sent the stone whizzing through the air. A second later, it smashed the goblet as the Queen lifted it to her lips.

The crowd went silent. The sound of breaking glass echoed round the bear pit, loud as a firework. To my amazement, the Queen didn't even flinch. She sat as if she was carved out of stone, holding the stem of the shattered goblet in her hand.

Suckley glared around him. Then he pointed to me and yelled in a cracked voice, "Seize that boy! He's a traitor!"

I pulled off my mask and threw my hat to the ground. My hair came undone and fell to my shoulders. "God save the Queen!" I shouted. Then everything happened at once.

Men from the Queen's Guard appeared out of nowhere. There were shouts and the clashing of swords. Suddenly Sam was behind Landemer, and two gentlemen had taken hold of my mother's arms on both sides. Henry of Orgon was pushed backwards and a guard grabbed him by the neck. The look on his face was one of complete and utter disbelief and, more than ever, I was sure he had known nothing of my mother's dealings.

Suckley spun round and saw Landemer for the first time. He started as if he had seen a ghost. As far as he knew, this baby-faced man was a servant. But here he was, dressed in the black-and-silver braid of a French aristocrat with a jewelled gold chain around his neck and a sword in his hand.

"Pierre Marchand!" howled Suckley, and I could hear the crazed terror in his voice. "What devilry is this?" With the instinct of an animal, he knew something was wrong. It was pitiful to watch him look in utter confusion from his hand to the smashed crystal stem that was still in the Queen's fingers.

"Poisoner!" cried Landemer.

"Never!" cried Suckley. He grabbed a goblet from the table and filled it with wine from the jug. Then he stumbled to his knees in front of the Queen and shouted, "I am your loyal servant, Majesty!" And he swallowed the wine in one gulp.

I learned later that the poison was larkspur. Suckley clutched at his throat as if a pair of invisible hands was throttling him. Then he crumpled and fell backwards, a bloody froth oozing from his mouth.

Two hours later, I stood with Richard and Arabella at the window of the flame-red room my mother had called her private chamber. Below us, we watched as two guards led her across the courtyard to a coach that would take her to the Tower of London.

I'm sure she knew we were there and that we would each be hoping that she would stop and look up at us. I thought of the wet morning Richard and I had been sent away from Croft Amber, when my mother had gone into the house without looking back before our coach had even turned in the yard.

This time I knew for certain that I would never see her again.

The guard opened the door of the coach. My mother pulled herself up on to the first steep step and disappeared into the gloom of the inside. She never looked up.

From the moment the Queen's Guard had arrested my mother, she had refused to speak a word. It had been Sam who made it known to the Queen that Henry of Orgon was innocent of treason. It had turned out to be exactly as I thought. Walsingham had never held any suspicions about him.

When I said as much to Sam, he'd kissed me and said that he couldn't abide cleverness in a woman and, before I could protest, he'd kissed me again.

As for Arabella, somehow my mother had found out about her marriage to Suckley and decided to get her revenge for the ruin of her plan in the only way left to her. Suckley had been no more than a vain, ignorant stooge, but she refused to clear his name, which damned Arabella as the widow of a traitor. It was a disgusting thing to do, but Arabella had refused to plead her case. Even if it meant being shut out of Court for ever, she wanted nothing to do with her mother. In the end, Sam and Uncle Charles wrote to the Queen and, within hours, the Queen made it known that Suckley was pardoned posthumously. In a gesture of kindness which no one expected, she received Arabella and gave her her blessing.

It was the best outcome that Arabella could have hoped for.

Now the three of us stood in silence as we watched the guards lock the coach door and saw the horses lean into their traces. There was a *crunch* of gravel and the coach disappeared up an avenue of oak trees.

"What of Landemer?" asked Arabella.

"In Oxford gaol," said Richard. "He'll be charged and taken to London tomorrow." He paused. "Orgon will stay here."

"And Bolton and his cronies?" I asked.

"They got away last night," Richard replied wearily. "I'd say they're halfway to France already." He shrugged. "Walsingham's men will get them soon enough."

There was an awkward silence, then Richard said to Arabella, "I know why you couldn't marry me. But for the life of me, I will never understand why you married Suckley."

I held my breath. I'd never expected Richard to ask. I guessed now that he was too exhausted to care about his own dignity, and just wanted to know the truth.

Arabella caught my eye and we looked at each other. I prayed she would hear the pain in his voice. She turned to Richard and said, "I married him because I am carrying his child. The Queen banished me from Court. He promised he could get me back into her favour and, in return, I let him seduce me. I will have to live with that mistake for the rest of my life."

I could hear Richard's mind turning like the workings of a clock. When he spoke at last, his voice was dead. "So you knew you were pregnant before I left for Portsmouth?"

Arabella nodded and looked at him unflinchingly. "I had to save my skin," she said. "I couldn't think of another way." Her eyes slipped sideways.

"You disgust me," said Richard, but there were tears in his eyes. I felt desperately sorry for him.

Arabella looked up. "I am truly sorry, Richard. I don't expect your forgiveness."

"Richard…" I held out my hand, but he pushed it away.

"You *knew*!" he shouted at me. "My own sister and you didn't tell me!"

270

"Don't blame Emerald," said Arabella. "She made me a promise and kept it. The fault is all mine."

"And you are well rewarded for it," said Richard icily. "Suckley's dead. You're a rich widow with the Queen's pardon." He buried his head in his hands. "Dear God! I am living in hell."

Arabella's voice was hardly there. "I tried to get rid of this child, Richard. Emerald found me and saved my life." She paused and looked at both us. "When I told Suckley the truth, wretch that he was, he agreed to marry me. Even though I was as loathsome to him as he was to me."

The three of us stood silent in the hall. Beyond the window came the bellowing of voices, and the creak and rumble of the carts and wagons beginning their long journeys south. In front of them our mother, locked in her coach, was on a longer voyage to the condemned cell and the executioner's block.

"Our mother was a terrible woman," said Richard at last. He sighed so deeply and so sadly, it was all I could do not to cry. He reached out and put his hand on Arabella's shoulder. "I forgive you, sister. Please God we can put this madness behind us."

The door opened and a servant came into the room and said, in a loud but respectful voice, "The Queen commands your presence in the Great Hall."

"Silence, my masters! Make way for Emerald St John!"

I don't know why I was so nervous at the thought of

speaking once more to the Queen. You would have thought I'd become quite used to her company. But every nerve in me felt on edge and knowing that Sam was there, and that we had barely spoken since my mother's arrest, only made things worse. I desperately wanted to be alone with him. At the last minute, Arabella had whispered in Richard's ear and he walked beside me so I could lean on his arm.

As we drew towards the end of the hall where the Queen sat surrounded by her ladies, Richard squeezed my hand. "I have not been a good brother to you," he whispered. "You deserve better."

I squeezed his hand in return and said, "You are the dearest brother in the world to me."

He let me go, and I walked the last few steps on my own.

"Emerald St John!" cried the usher.

The Queen waved away her ladies and I swept a deep curtsey in front of her.

"Come near me, child," she said, and pointed to a stool at her feet.

I sat down and prayed that my heart would stop hammering.

"It seems I owe you my life, child," said the Queen. She reached out and touched me with her long fingers. The cloth of her sleeves was encrusted with gold and chips of turquoise. "In return I want to offer you a life with me." Her eyes held mine. "If it pleases you, Emerald, you shall come to London and live at Court." She paused and let her hand rest on my shoulder. "You would do me a great honour if you accepted."

It was as if the floor had opened up in front of me and I was about to fall through the blackest hole to the middle of the earth. I didn't want a life at Court. I wanted to marry Sam and live somewhere, anywhere, as long as we were on our own and there was a roof over our heads. A piece of canvas would do.

My thoughts must have been written all over my face.

"I see my offer does not please you," said the Queen in a low voice.

I thought I was going to faint and fall off the stool. "Your Majesty—" I whispered.

"No matter," interrupted the Queen. But she didn't sound angry. I followed her eyes as she looked across the room to where Sam was watching us, his body taut as a spring.

"Ah, Viscount Pemberton," she murmured, half to herself and half to me. "I had forgotten about him." She clicked her tongue. Then she leaned forward and whispered, "Do you love that man, child?"

"With all my heart, Your Majesty," I croaked.

"Can he provide for you?"

It was the last question I had expected and the shock of it made me remember the purse of gold nuggets I had given Sam at Hawkstone to invest in his expedition with Richard. There had been no time to ask him if the venture had been a success.

"I don't know, Your Majesty."

The Queen saw something in my face. "Explain yourself, child."

So I did. And when she had heard my story to the end, she clapped her hands delightedly.

She signalled to a servant, and Sam was led over to join us. He was dressed in a green velvet doublet embroidered with black silk, and his blond hair hung in silky curls from his head. He had never looked so handsome and all I wanted was to touch him.

I looked away so neither of them could see the blush rising in my cheeks.

"Are you as good a pirate as you are a spy, sir?" demanded the Queen. "This young woman is dear to me, and I would see she is well looked after."

Sam tried to hide his surprise, but it didn't work. "A thousand pardons, Your Majesty," he spluttered. "I—"

"Come, sir," said the Queen in a teasing voice. "You may tell me the truth about your so-called expedition. I approve of men who make their own fortunes." She nodded to me as if she was taking my part.

"Emerald tells me she put forty gold nuggets with you. How does she fare as an investor, sir?"

I had never seen Sam look so discomfited and I almost burst out laughing.

The Queen took pity on him. "Fie, sir," she said. "You know I cannot condone the actions of a pirate – but I can praise the courage of a sailor if our neighbours' treasure ships get the worst of it."

Sam recovered himself. "Our expedition was more successful that we could ever have hoped for, Majesty," he said. "Emerald's gold has increased a hundredfold." He turned to me. "My only regret is that this is the first chance I have had to tell her."

There was a silence for a moment then the Queen smiled. "I congratulate you both. You for your seamanship, sir. And you, Emerald, for the canniness of your investment."

Sam took my hand and it was as if a streak of lightning passed between us. Then he looked into my eyes and I knew what he was going to say. He bowed in front of the Queen and I dropped a low curtsey. "May we have your permission to marry, Your Majesty?" he asked in the lowest voice I could imagine.

"You may," said the Queen shortly. She signalled for us to rise. "Even though I suspect you would have run off together in any case."

She opened an embroidered purse that hung from her girdle and put something in my hand. "A gift," she murmured. "I want you to accept it."

It was a fabulous emerald ring set within a circle of diamonds. I opened my mouth to thank her, but the Queen shook her head. "It is a small thing in exchange for a life," she said.

Meg held the ring in her hand and sniffed the emerald. "Right fragrant," she said. "Even smells like Her Holiness. Can I try it on?"

"Don't be silly, Meg," said Sarah. 'Your fingers are far too small – and dirty, too, I expect." She swept the last of the rushes into a corner of the room and shook the bedclothes that were hanging out of the window.

Meg licked her thumb and held it up. "It'll fit this," she said in a plaintive voice. "Please, miss. I ain't never worn an emerald before."

Sarah laughed. "Nor have I."

Meg pushed the ring on to her thumb and went over to the window to see it in the dawn light. "Look, there's Arabella leaving!" she cried.

I ran to the window to wave, but Arabella had already climbed into the shiny black coach that would take her to Suckley's estate in Macclesfield. She had decided to live there, and her father intended to join her.

I caught Sarah's eye. Apart from Sam, she was the only person who knew what Arabella had told me when we'd said goodbye.

"I have made over Hawkstone to you and your heirs," she'd said. "Father and I agree that you are the nearest to a daughter that Frances ever had and she would want you to have it."

It was true that Hawkstone was a home to me, but when I realised that now I would never have to leave it, I understood how much it meant to me.

Arabella had held out her arms and we had stood and hugged each other. "I owe you everything," she'd whispered. "You are my dearest sister and I thank God for you."

"Is it true you and Mr Sam's goin' to live at Hawkstone

when you's married?" asked Meg now. She licked the ring as if it was a lump of coloured sugar.

I stared at her. "Who told you that?" I asked.

"Hetty," said Sarah, shaking her head.

Meg's face went white. "Don't tell 'er I told. She'd kick me into the gutter if she found out."

There was a pause. Then Meg said, "An' Tom told me about the bear, miss."

I shook my head and smiled. It was to have been a surprise for Meg. Sam had asked Tom to look at the old bear's paw to see if the wound would heal. Tom said it would and so we agreed to take the creature back to Hawkstone with us to keep Molly company, as the two bears had become inseparable.

The whole thing was to have been a surprise for Meg who had become very fond of the old bear.

I turned to Sarah. "Seems like you can't keep *anything* secret around here."

"I'm glad to hear it, miss," said Sarah, smiling. "I'd say we've had enough secrets to last a year of Januaries."

I smiled back. "I'd say you're right."

As I took the ring from Meg and put it on my finger, I thought of Sam and the love I felt for him.

Beyond the window, a great yellow sun rose above pink-and gold-clouds and I watched as morning light spread over the land.

My new life was beginning, and the purest joy filled my heart.

KAREN WALLACE

Shortlisted for the **Guardian Fiction Award**

"funny, perceptive, moving and utterly absorbing… Brilliant.
A *Swallows and Amazons* for the 21st century."
Michael Morpurgo

KAREN WALLACE

"Wallace writes this poignant novel with a breezy stylishness
that compels you to read on until all its mysteries are solved."
The Sunday Times, Children's Book of the Week

"I raced through *Climbing a Monkey Puzzle Tree*
with huge enjoyment." Jacqueline Wilson

KAREN WALLACE

"Clever and original... this does something quite unexpected with Peter Pan." *The Sunday Times*

"A stunningly good idea, well executed." *Observer*

"Quite the most intelligent book I've read in a long while."
Celia Rees

KAREN WALLACE

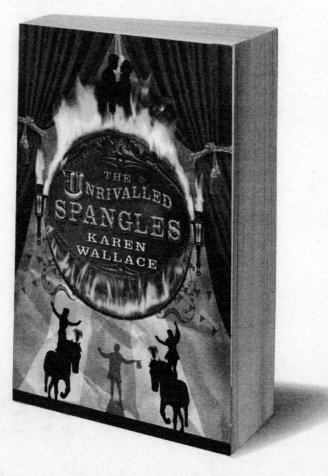

"an enjoyable story, with plenty of drama. Read it for the sheer
exuberance of the circus and a superbly drawn historical setting."
Nicola Morgan, *The Guardian*

"Roll up and be entertained." *The Sunday Times*

"Love, death, drama and conflict of every sort... fascinating."
Adele Geras, *The Times*